OPUS MURDER

A JILL QUINT, MD, SERIES MYSTERY

ALEC PECHE

GBSW PUBLISHING

I want to thank Grace and Kathy for helping me make this the most polished manuscript. I would also like to thank Tim Fayle for his suggestions on how to make the murder weapon better – only an author can make a statement like that.

Parts of this story are genuine. I was in Toronto two years ago and did sit in a church to hear a free noon recital. I listened to the concert, and that inspired me to write this story. I also spent many a summer vacation as a child on a lake outside of Toronto, so the story is a mixture of decades-old and recent experiences in Canada.

CHAPTER 1

Jill Quint, MD, forensic pathologist, relaxed in the historic church in downtown Toronto. The church was quiet and dark from the wood that lined the walls and sanctuary. The smell of beeswax accelerated the sense of calm. She, Angela, Marie, and Jo had taken time out from their sightseeing to relax and listen to the free noontime recital they'd read about on a travel site. As a team, they had zero musical ability; instead, their skills were in solving murder. They had additional friends and family on this trip. Henrik, a former client, and now Marie's love interest had joined them from Germany. Jill's partner, Nathan from California, Angela's mother - Hope from Wisconsin, and Jo's friend, Jack from Green Bay. It was just the women inside the church as the three men were exploring craft distilleries.

Nikita Chernov, the pianist for this recital, bowed to the audience then sat down on the bench, pushing his coattails out of the way. He moved his head to work out the stiffness, brushed his hair away from his eyes, sat up straight, and placed his hands on the keyboard ready to play the first selection that he'd memorized for this recital. The music was so mesmerizing that Jill felt her attention drifting off to somewhere beyond this church.

The recital continued as the pianist began the third of four pieces. Jill looked at the program, which said this would be Beethoven's Sonata in A Flat Major, Opus 110. Jill liked classical music, but she could never guess who the composer was behind a piece. She was just not well versed enough in the various composers' works. As she sat in the church, she researched what A Flat Major meant in music, and decided it was a piece that would revolve around specific keys in a particular pitch. Around her were aficionados of the piano listening deeply with heads swaying to the pianist's interpretation of the composer's work.

She tuned back into the music, and the pianist as the music took on more emotion and rose to a crescendo. It was exciting, and she wondered where the music was going. The pianist seemed to be talking to himself as the piece gained momentum. Arms and fingers were sliding across the keys. Softly, twinkling the keys, then a full thrashing of the keyboard. He would straighten up before plunging his fingers down on the keyboard. She watched for awhile, trying to guess whether he was counting beats in his head or listening for a particular musical note. She should have researched which pieces would be played that day and listened to them before this recital, so she would appreciate the technique she was hearing.

And then suddenly, without realizing it, she was out of her church pew and racing toward the pianist to the startled gasps of onlookers and the sudden silence in the church. Jill hopped up on stage, kneeling beside the pianist where he lay on the floor of the sanctuary, his eyes closed, his feet in the air stuck on the over-turned piano bench, a red stain spreading rapidly around the edge of an ice spear or arrow sticking out of his chest.

It was stuck in his chest, the ice deadly and melting. Although it was losing its killing essence already as the aim was on target.

Jill felt others crowd around her as she reached for the man's pulse. It was rapid, and the bloodstain spread across his pristine white shirt under a black suit coat. Jill thought the man had minutes to live as the arrow seemed to have pierced his heart. She made brief contact with his eyes before they closed forever. There was panic in his eyes. Wild panic. Panic knowing his life was draining away. Draining away with each drop of blood staining his shirt.

The pianist would bleed out before an ambulance arrived even as she heard several people talking on their cell phones to emergency personnel. Jill looked for Angela wanting the photographer to take pictures of the scene and the victim. She made eye contact and motioned snapping a picture with her hand, and Angela nodded. She looked back at the pianist as she heard someone say close by, "Should we remove the arrow... or just let it...melt?"

Jill shook her head and replied, "Let's just keep him comfortable and hold his hands in support until an ambulance arrives. I'm a doctor."

The spectator nodded gravely, seeming to understand the message behind Jill's words, and took the man's other hand in hers and joined Jill in the vigil. They heard with relief, sirens in the distance coming closer. The man's hand grip grew weaker, and his pulse slowed. She was relieved when the first responders arrived and scooped the man onto a gurney while trying to work on him at the same time. The arrow had shrunk in size and might disappear by the time the pianist reached the hospital. She heard that the hospital was just blocks away, and perhaps they could perform a miracle for the pianist. Jill sighed and looked down at herself, glad that she didn't have any blood on her hands or clothing. She had managed not to kneel in it. She stood up and walked over to the pipes hanging down from the organ, knowing that was where the arrow had come. The organ pipes were fixed in place, and she bent closer to look behind them.

She jumped abruptly when she heard a voice behind her ask, "What are you doing, don't touch anything!"

She turned around to face the uniform of a woman wearing the Toronto Metropolitan Police insignia on her sleeve. Her attire consisted of a dark navy blue shirt, a bomber jacket, and a bright yellow vest with 'police' marked on it. The uniform was complete with cargo pants with a red stripe, and a bicycle helmet. She must have arrived by bike. Jill liked the thought that bikes were faster than cars sometimes when arriving at a crime scene.

"Hello, I'm Jill Quint. I'm a licensed private investigator and forensic pathologist from California. I was first on the scene when the pianist was struck by the ice arrow. I was just examining where the arrow originated from."

"Stay right here, please, and don't touch anything," the officer said, making eye contact with Jill before turning away to walk over to another officer.

Jill liked the politeness of the officer. Canadians were renowned for their polite and friendly behavior.

She stood looking around the church at the activity. She could see that the police had blocked all exits and were interviewing audience members. Angela was snapping the occasional photo. Jo, Marie, and Hope were patiently sitting on their pew, waiting for officers to get around to interviewing them. Jill wondered if any of them had texted the men to tell them what they were involved with inside the church. They might be there for several hours. As her gaze was sweeping the room, she could see the bike officer speaking with a man wearing a gray suit with a blue tie. The man must be one of the detectives that had just arrived on the case. They both looked over at her while the detective listened to the patrol officer.

The detective started walking toward where Jill stood in the sanctuary. She could see a wide variety of officers taking statements from recital attendees. She was pleased she would be talking to the detective.

"Ma'am, I'm Detective Peter Ireland of the Toronto Metropolitan Police Homicide Squad. I understand you're a key witness and that you have some specialized training. Can you confirm that you were the first person to attend our victim?"

"Yes. I was out of my seat and running for this stage as soon as I saw the arrow hit the pianist. I checked his pulse and held his hand, but I considered his injuries likely fatal. Has the hospital been able to save him?"

"No, ma'am. We officially have a murder on our hands."

"Have you retrieved the weapon from the victim's body yet?"

"Ma'am, I'm not at liberty to share the details of this case with you. I understand an ice arrow killed him and that once his body temperature melted it, all of our evidence went away."

"I wouldn't be too sure about that. I believe there was a tip on the front of the arrow, but I admit the arrow flashed by quickly. Anatomically, it makes sense to me as I would not necessarily expect an ice arrow to make it through the fibers of the pianist's shirt, let alone kill him. I'm sure your coroner will discover the tip when he or she does the autopsy."

"Would you please provide me with your identity, training, and where you're from?"

She handed the detective her passport and said, "I'm Dr. Jill Quint. I'm a licensed physician in California with a sub-specialty in Forensics and Toxicology. I'm also a Private Investigator licensed by the state, and I provide second opinions on the cause of death. Since I left the crime lab, I've helped various law enforcement agencies including, the FBI, Interpol, and most recently, the Italian Polizia, solve murders. If you want references, I can provide them. My team is here on vacation, and we were enjoying the recital until the pianist's death happened."

The detective had been furiously writing Jill's information down as she recited her professional history and gave a contact number at the FBI where he could check her references. The detective couldn't believe that such a qualified person was on-scene when a murder occurred. He snapped a picture of her passport; he would have to check out her references and then go from there.

Once the detective stopped writing, Jill asked, "Have you notified the American Embassy yet? That will bring in the FBI."

"Is our victim an American? How do you know that?" he asked suspiciously.

"It says in the recital program that our victim's name is Nikita Chernov, and he's a renowned American pianist."

"Somehow, that detail escaped my attention, just a moment," he said with a sigh.

Whoops, someone forgot to tell the detective this crucial detail. He stepped out of Jill's hearing and took out a mobile phone to make a call.

She took the opportunity to check in with her friends, and she could see a patrol officer was interviewing them. Good, they could get out of there sooner than she expected. She turned back to the organ pipes trying to determine where the killer was positioned. He or she must have brought the arrow or multiple arrows in a cooler as it would have melted or at least lost its shape while the shooter was waiting for the perfect moment in the music. The shooter also had to be experienced with aiming only for the heart, and they had to be strong enough to pull the string back far enough to strike Nikita's chest hard enough to go through his clothing and skin to pierce the heart.

Jill looked at her watch and knew it was time to move on. They were expected to meet the guys ten minutes ago for lunch. Her phone was in her purse back on the pew, so she couldn't text Nathan. She looked over at her friends and noticed that Marie was looking at her, she gestured to her watch and then held out her thumb and pinky fingers imitating the shape of the phone. Marie seemed to understand her question. She nodded and pointed to herself and imitated texting on her phone. Jill relaxed, happy that the men wouldn't worry when they didn't show up on time. She looked over at the detective and saw that he finished his call and was returning to her side.

"You're quite well known with your FBI."

"Well, I have worked with them on a few cases," Jill said.

"Yes, I guess they think so highly of you that they will reimburse us if we hire you and your team as consultants."

"Oh, but we're on vacation here. We planned to go to Montréal and Québec City after spending a few days between here and Niagara Falls."

"Yeah, well, your government wants you to assist the Toronto Metropolitan Police."

"Okay, let me talk to my friends. Unlike most cases, we have more friends and family with us on this vacation. Let me see what everyone thinks," Jill said as she stepped from the sanctuary to approach her friends in the pews.

"The guys know we're going to be late?" Jill said.

"Yeah, they're waiting outside the church for us," Marie said. "This was so weird. This was the first person I saw murdered in front of us, and still, I feel like I didn't see anything. I thought I'd be a better witness."

Jill looked over at Hope and said, "Sorry, Mom, didn't mean to have you exposed to violence on our vacation."

"That's okay, dear. Did the poor man live?"

"No, I could tell the arrow pierced a critical component of his heart – either a major artery or a chamber as he was nearly dead by the time the ambulance arrived."

Hope bowed her head and made the sign of the cross, saying a quick, silent prayer for the dead musician. Then she looked up and said, "What now, does that policeman want our help solving the case?"

Jill gave a surprised look at Angela's mother. She'd hoped to shield her from the nastiness of murder. She was further surprised to hear the word, 'our'.

"Actually, he said the American Embassy relayed that the FBI wants us to assist the Toronto police. I said I would talk to you guys first and the men outside as we're here on vacation to relax and have fun, not to sit in a hotel room and do computer searches."

"Well, there are more of us than on your usual case, so perhaps we can solve it quickly and not miss Montréal or Québec City. Marie, Angela, and I have been to Niagara Falls before. Besides from what Angela has said, you bear the workload of these cases. How do you feel about giving up your vacation time?" Hope asked, a twinkle in her eye.

Her friends grinning, Jo said knowingly, "She loves these cases. Loves the pursuit of truth and justice. Are they going to pay us? Maybe we could move up to a fancy suite in a swanky hotel and drink lots of beer and wine while we solve this case!"

"Henrik might enjoy being on a case from the start," Marie suggested.

"Nathan will roll his eyes, then take off and explore wineries and cook for us while we investigate," Angela said.

"This will be like one of those newfangled mystery dinners, only sadly it will be the real thing. Who Killed Nikita at the Oriental Theater," Hope said, and Angela leaned in to hug her mother.

"Okay. I'll ask the detectives to let our menfolk in, and we'll go to work," Jill said.

Detective Ireland had been watching the women trying to guess what they were going to do. The agent he'd talked to at the FBI had given the team of women high marks for being helpful. Furthermore, they didn't talk to the media. He never worked with anyone outside of the Metropolitan Police other than his colleagues at the Ontario Provincial Police and the RCMP. Of course, he never investigated a murder of anyone other than a Canadian. And this murder had such a dramatic flare to it. He looked up from his notebook, where he was writing his initial thoughts about the case, as Dr. Quint approached him.

"We agreed to help at least for a couple of days. We have three friends outside of this church that we would like brought in as they will help us with the case. You'll be getting help from one of the biggest security experts in the world. He'll be able to unlock the victim's cellphone in under ten minutes."

The detective felt a headache coming on as he wondered how he was going to control eight Americans and still manage this case. He waved one of the patrol officers over and asked him to escort the doctor outside and have her identify three men to bring inside. As she left his side, he took notes on what he wanted to say to the group once they assembled inside the church. His Detective-Sergeant was on his way to the church as this investigation was fast getting complicated.

Jill spotted Nathan, Henrik, and Jack leaning against a bus stop shelter outside the church. They straightened up and began walking toward her when she appeared with the officer. She met them at the base of the steps of the church and Nathan reached out to engulf her in a hug.

"Everything okay?" he asked.

"We're all alive and well, but a man is dead and the FBI has asked us to assist the Metropolitan Police. The ladies voted to comply with the FBI's request, so we've got work to do."

"Do you have a phone that needs unlocking?" Henrik asked, rubbing his hands together.

Jill laughed, "I just bragged to the detective about your phone unlocking skills, so I'll assume we'll have a phone for you."

"Is the FBI paying you for your time?" Nathan asked.

"Why?" Jill asked, suspiciously.

"Why don't all of you go inside, and I'll arrange new digs for everyone and a kitchen for me."

"Did Angela text you?" Jill asked Nathan with a raised eyebrow.

"No, I'm just trying to get you your usual space set up."

"Love you, Sweetie," Jill said, leaning into to kiss Nathan. "You know me so well."

Henrik pulled out his phone and said to them, "Just a moment and walked away from them." He had a quick conversation and then returned.

"Nathan, I took care of the lodging. My hotel is going to place you all in the Presidential Suite, which is on the same floor as my suite. There will be enough bedrooms for everyone and a kitchen for Nathan or room service if he's not in the mood to cook. They're expecting you, and you can begin moving everyone's luggage over."

"Ah, guys. The FBI is going to pay, but it will be enough for a conference room at a one-star hotel. I need a cheaper solution."

"Tell you what Jill, if it makes you feel better, you can pass on your fee from the FBI to me, and I'll make up the difference to cover the hotel bill. This investigation might be a great solution for my recent boredom."

"Thank you for your generosity. I'll warn you there will be a lot of boring internet searches and chasing down of tedious details. The only glamour might be the wine that Nathan chooses each night."

Henrik leaned in and raised Jill's hand, kissing the back of it, "We're all good. Let's go inside and get started."

Jill thought for a moment longer and couldn't come up with a reasonable argument against Henrik's move, so she shrugged, and lead the way up the stairs into the church. Nathan followed to retrieve Angela and Jo's room keys, and Jack left with Nathan to handle the transfer of luggage.

Jill walked back inside the church and noted that nearly all of the other civilians were cleared away. Those that remained huddled in a small group out of the hearing range of the few civilians undergoing interviews. She made introductions and relayed what Nathan and Jack were planning to do. The detective introduced new arrivals as well, agent Susan Garrett from the FBI, Detective-Sargent Balaji Hassan, and Detective Chloe Kim.

CHAPTER 2

The group recapped the details of the murder they saw unfold in front of their eyes for the newcomers. For the benefit of the officers, Jill also detailed some of her prior work with the FBI and international law enforcement agencies. She then described what each of her team members would do.

"As you know, I'm a forensic pathologist, so I would like to join your pathologist when they do the autopsy. Marie will begin working on a dossier of sorts as she collects anything the man has ever posted online. Jo will review his finances and those of anyone connected to him, while Angela will process the photographs she took both before and after the recital. Henrik will unlock his phone for you and us. Henrik and Jack will review any security systems and cameras located around the church. Hope isn't normally on one of our cases, so she'll use her sharp mind to ask questions we haven't thought of. We're setting up a suite in the Crown Royal Hotel, and we'll keep track of our findings in a series of whiteboards or butcher paper – we'll have to see what the suite has."

"We have many of our department experts that will be doing

the same things you've described," Detective Ireland stated. "I'll see about arranging your attendance to the victim's autopsy."

"How soon will you be sharing information you've collected from this scene?" Jill asked.

The detective looked puzzled by her question. He hadn't said they planned to go over the victim's belongings and look for evidence. The puzzlement must have shown on his face.

Jill added, "The victim's cell phone, local video footage. When will that be shared with us?"

"Ah, we'll make copies of the video footage within the hour, but you won't see the cell phone until tomorrow."

"Where is the cell phone at this moment?" Jill asked, thinking she might convince Henrik to go to the police station to unlock the phone for them.

"It's in the crime lab in Toronto," replied Detective Kim.

"How long have they had the phone?" Henrik asked.

The detective looked at her watch and then replied, "About thirty minutes."

"If they don't crack the phone within the next thirty minutes, please send a car to me to the Crown Royal Hotel. If you fetch it, I'll have it unlocked today," Henrik said.

The detective-sergeant looked at Henrik as if only now remembering that he was from Germany after hearing the accent in his voice, and so he asked, knowing it was not vital to them solving the case, but curiosity grabbed his tongue.

"How does a German citizen get to know this team of Americans?" asked Hassan.

"They solved the murder of my wife three years ago and captured a monstrous serial killer. Now I try to help them when I can, and we are friends."

"Sorry to hear about the death of your wife. I don't have a resume on you, sir. Can you tell me what your background is?"

"I'm the CEO of Klein Industries. Your government has purchased several security systems from my company, and I maintain your RCMP database in my cloud. I also hack computers for fun and to make sure that my company's computers are a few steps ahead of the hackers from the dark web."

"Dr. Quint, you've assembled a powerful team here. No wonder your government has such respect for your work. Give me a moment while I check on that cell phone, and find out when the autopsy is going to occur."

With this last statement, the detectives stepped away from the pews that Jill's team had been sitting in.

Jill looked at Henrik and said, "I forgot to ask you men when I met you outside. How was the distillery tour?"

"As you Americans say, 'we were feeling no pain' when we made our way back in your direction, but the news of what happened here had a very sobering effect on all of us."

"Well, once we're all comfortable in the suite, and after you've unlocked the phone, you can resume your spirits tasting," Jill said with smiling eyes. "After our distillery tour of Scotland, I'm cured from exploring whiskey flavors. I'll stick with beer and wine."

She looked up as the detectives returned to their pew.

"The phone is on its way here, as soon as you unlock it, we would like you to make a copy for your team and return the original to us. We're going to have you sign some paperwork referring to the chain of custody of the phone, so we don't get into trouble when this case goes to trial."

"No worries," replied Henrik.

"Dr. Quint, the autopsy will start at 8 am tomorrow. I'll meet you at your hotel lobby at 7:30. That will give us time to get there and get gowned by the start time."

Jill nodded and asked, "Should we reconvene this evening and share what we learned?"

The detectives looked uncomfortable, so Jill added, "We expect you to share your findings with us. If this is just a one-way street from us to you, then Agent Garrett should inform the FBI and the consulate that we decided we don't want to work under those conditions, and we'll resume our vacation."

Garrett looked at her Canadian colleagues and said, "I'd advise Detective-Sargent Hassan that we need to have a clear statement of the ground rules. My colleagues in the United States have informed me that this team in front of you is one of our best assets outside of the Bureau. If you don't really want our help solving this murder inquiry, then say so at the start. Our government will be hounding you daily for results, and we'll inform the media that you rejected the assistance of one of the best tools the FBI has for solving murders."

There was silence as the Hassan weighed the agent's words.

"I've been with the Metro for going on twenty years, and I've never used civilians in an investigation. I hear what you're saying about your best and brightest being in front of us. We're going to stumble in our relationship with Dr. Quint and the FBI, but as a detective, our goal is to get the murderer off the streets of Canada, if indeed he or she is still here within the country. We would appreciate your help and we'll schedule a meeting at say nine tonight?"

"That will be fine. Our suite will have meeting space, according to Henrik, so we can meet there or at the detective's division. Let us know what you would prefer," Jill offered, trying to deescalate the tension.

"We'll let you know the meeting location by five," Hassan said, looking at his watch.

A patrol officer entered carrying a package and walked over to Detective Ireland, reaching out to hand the package to him. The two officers signed something on the front; then the patrol officer waited while the detective opened the package and pulled out a cell phone. Jill noticed he did so without gloves on, so it must have already been dusted for fingerprints.

Detective Ireland handed the phone to Henrik, and said,

"You'll need to sign here that you've had custody of the phone," as he pointed to a place on the package.

Henrik smiled as he saw the phone. It wasn't an iPhone, so he thought he'd have it unlocked in no time. He took his own phone out, and used something on the phone to read something on the victim's phone. He hit the screens of both phones while everyone watched in silence. In no time he unlocked the victim's phone, and he showed the screen to the detectives. He then made another change and again took his phone and aimed it at the unlocked phone.

"What are you doing now?" asked Detective Kim, worry in her voice. She didn't want this stranger destroying a key source of their investigation.

"I changed the phone's passcode to 'detective', and now I'm copying the contents of his phone to my cloud so that we'll have a copy, and you can take this phone back to your laboratory."

Hassan smiled and asked, "Would you be interested in a job in our lab?"

"Thank you, sir, but no. I'm working on a technology for police forces to unlock phones, but I have concerns about its uses, and the damage it can do to the world. Until I figure out the safe deployment of the technology, I won't be sharing it."

They all nodded with the understanding of what this kind of technology could do in the hands of corrupt governments or police forces. People's lives could be destroyed if anyone had open access to their phones.

"Given the financial information on many phones, including my own, your technology could be a weapon of mass destruction to the world's financial institutions. Henrik, I don't think you should ever release that technology to anyone," Jo said, as her friends were nodding in agreement with her every word.

Henrik handed the phone back to Detective Ireland, taking a moment to sign the chain of custody form.

"Is there anything more we need to know? Did anything come

in while we have been talking?" Jill asked.

The detectives took another look at their phones and shook their heads 'no'.

Jill and her group slowly walked up the aisle to exit the church leaving the detectives and agent to discuss whatever they wanted outside of their presence.

They hailed two taxis to take them to their new residence after checking with Nathan and Jack to make sure they were installed in the new suite. It would likely be a level of luxury they hadn't seen since they stayed at Henrik's house outside of Stuttgart. When they pulled up to the Crown Royal Hotel, Jill knew her team was in for a treat. Angela's mom would probably not be pleased with the cost of the luxury they were about to step into, but at least everyone would have a good night's sleep, and the hotel would have good security.

Key cards were distributed to them to access the special suite, and Jack was waiting at the open door to greet them. There were two levels of living space to the suite with amazing views of Toronto.

"We have everyone's luggage stowed in their room, but first Nathan ordered up a meal from the hotel kitchen since we missed it due to the incident at the church. Each bedroom has a bathroom, or you can use the kitchen or bar sink to wash your hands."

After a short pause, everyone scattered to their rooms and were back out at the dining table ready for sandwiches, salads, soup, and beer and wine.

"I'm starved. Thanks for taking care of the food. Are you going to cook here or order from the kitchen?" Jill said, looking around the only small room in the suite – the kitchen.

"A little of both, I think. I'm going shopping after lunch, so if everyone will put their favorites on a list for all three daily meals, that would be great."

"I won't be any help with your computer searches, so I'll share kitchen duty with Nathan," Hope said.

Angela hugged her mother while Marie looked around for exercise equipment, "Is there a treadmill in this suite?" she asked.

"There is one on the upstairs balcony," Jo said.

Marie gave her a thumbs up. The suite she was sharing with Henrik was smaller and didn't have exercise equipment. She thought she would be spending a lot more time in this suite, than her own and she had keys for both suites.

"Hope, you'll be very helpful on this case. You watched the murder happen. That will give you some insight. Furthermore, you're a smart woman, and we value your thoughts on the case. Just ask Nathan, he'll occasionally half-listen to us discuss a case, and he'll lob a thought at us that causes us to look differently at the case, and then we'll solve it."

"You're too kind, dear. We'll see."

They moved on to describing for the men what had gone on inside the church and the subsequent interactions with the Canadian police. Jack enjoyed hearing Henrik's story of unlocking the phone.

Jill found a recording of the Beethoven piece they listened to at the time of the murder, and they listened to the crescendo several times.

"Wouldn't it be great if the Canadian Police find the suspect today? However, if they don't, we need to organize ourselves. Nathan and Hope are going to keep us well-fed and interject at various times to point our attention in the right direction. Henrik and Jack are going to review and enhance any video surveillance we receive from the police later today. Jo is going to look into the finances of Nikita Chernov. Angela is going to process all of her photographs and share them with Henrik and Jack. I think you should also interview the person in the church that arranged for this musician at this recital. Marie is going to prepare a dossier on Nikita. I'll start a murder board going on the walls. I'm going to research using an ice arrow as a murder weapon – it sounds like a weapon from <u>Game of Thrones</u>. I wonder if it was on that show?"

"They had an ice sword, but not an ice arrow," Jo said.

"Well, that's a start on that research. Maybe if I watch a few episodes, I can understand how they kept the sword from melting."

"I don't remember that being an issue, but then the kingdom suffered a long winter. Let's just say it looked cold on the set. I think it was meant to be more symbolic. The family melted the ice sword into two different swords to represent the fracturing of the family."

"Hmmm, I wonder if it means the same thing here? Maybe the melting arrow represents the decline of something," Jill said.

"That a pretty wild theory. What is <u>Game of Thrones</u> – was it a movie?" Henrik asked.

"Nearly all of our motives for murder are not what we think at the beginning of a case. <u>Game of Thrones</u> is a television series based on the novel by R.R. Martin."

Marie looked up from her computer and said, "You must be out of touch with the Millennials as it's all the rage. I just checked, and it was broadcasted in Germany. Not to worry Henrik, I didn't watch it either. I don't much like dystopian stories."

"Jo and I watched every episode of every season. It's pretty dark," Jack said. "Toronto doesn't feel very dystopian, so it wouldn't come to mind as a setting or motive for this murder. On television, they don't have to worry about melting swords."

Jill nodded and started work on the murder board. There were dry-erase boards in the suite's dining room, which the hotel created to serve the dual purpose of being a dining room and conference room. She sketched the church's interior, including the pews, altar, organ, pipes, sanctuary, and the likely route that the murderer took. She also gave thought to the original length of the arrow and the size of the cooler required so that it didn't melt. The pianist had been killed some thirty-five minutes into the performance, so when did the archer arrive? Just before the arrow was released or perhaps even before the concert started?

She started a parking lot of questions: When did the archer arrive? Was there a tip on the arrow? How far in advance was the musical program confirmed? What space existed between the pipes? What was the size of the original arrow? Jill would add to the list once they brainstormed later in the day. She was just anxious to get everyone moving in the same direction for the investigation.

"As we don't have any video yet, I'll help Jo and Marie gather information. I probably can find and access Mr. Chernov's bank accounts faster than you can, Jo," Henrik suggested.

"Of that I have no doubt," she replied with a smile, looking up from her laptop. "I'll waste time looking for information through legitimate sources while you can just abscond with the data before anyone notices that someone is viewing their private information."

"I really don't have the magical powers you all ascribe to me," Henrik said, trying to look modest and failing. He'd helped Jill before with requests for her cases, but he hadn't been in the heart of an investigation since his wife had been murdered a couple of years ago in Belgium. He was enjoying using his computer science skills to help track down a murderer. It was like having permission to do illegal things on the internet. It tested what he thought he knew about himself in terms of finding information, but there was a purpose behind it. He was also enjoying the experience of being an equal partner in a mission rather than a CEO of a multinational corporation.

Henrik looked up from his computer to find everyone's eyes, but Hope's, on him with doubtful expressions about his statement.

Nathan brought a glass of Riesling over to his friend and said, "You're outnumbered. Better to fold. Just advice to a bud."

Nathan's comment broke the restless atmosphere into relaxation as everyone put their heads down with a smile to begin their work on the curious case of Nikita Chernov, pianist extraordinaire, and now dead by a most unusual murder weapon of an ice arrow.

It was late afternoon after Nathan returned from grocery shopping when Jill checked in with everyone to check their readiness to share their findings and talk through their next steps. She also thought they probably all needed a walk outside. Maybe someone could suggest a destination to walk to, or perhaps they would go out to eat. The Toronto police sent Jill copies of the street videos around the church, and in the last half an hour, videos from inside the church had arrived.

She'd viewed those videos inside the church with Jack and Henrik, and nothing immediately caught her attention and so she'd left the footage to the two men to study in a frame by frame detail. Jill had this faint hope that the murderer would have a sign around their neck that said, "I did it", and then they could all resume their vacation, but she knew in her heart it wasn't going to be that easy.

"Marie, why don't you start by telling us about our victim?"

"Thanks to researching our victim, I know more about training for a classical pianist. Nikita Chernov was twenty-five years old. Born in Nizhny, Novgorod, Russia, he started playing the piano at age five. Both of his parents were musicians, though neither reached the heights of popularity that Nikita did. He entered competitions at the junior level and then at the senior level, including winning the top prizes in Sydney, New Orleans, and Singapore. He also won the Cliburn at both the junior and senior levels. According to reviewers, 'he has an evenness of tone in every finger, clear articulation, sensitivity to phrasing and rhythmic accuracy'. I have no training in piano, so I'm not sure what any of those comments mean other than to say he was considered brilliant."

"So what's a high caliber and an accomplished piano player like that doing providing free concerts in churches in Canada?" asked Nathan.

"Well, that's a good question that I asked myself after I looked at the tenth award he'd won. I think the answer is a combination of his mental burnout and a decline in audiences for classical music. There are just too many pianists for the relatively few roles worldwide. It gets a little worse every year as more of the audience dies off as the audience skews older.

"Winning all of these awards and accolades went to his head by the age of nineteen. On top of that, he'd been raised in the restrictive Russian environment and then had access to the world on tour. I read comments about him as he became impossible to build a concert around. He wouldn't like the conductor or his orchestra. One time he became so upset with a piano that he pulled out a pocket knife and cut the strings. When word of his temper tantrums hit the music world, he was no longer booked for concerts. He returned to Russia for four to five years, then started playing church concerts and the like making a slow comeback starting with this past summer."

"When and why did he become an American citizen?" Jo asked.

"That's an interesting question, and my conclusion is he's not an American."

"Yes, but the flier said he was an American," Jill said.

"Neither Henrik nor I could find that he was a U.S. Citizen."

"That's interesting. I wonder why Nikita would lie about that? I guess that means the embassy is going to back away as well as the FBI. I would think they'll tell us that tonight. Let's see if they bring that up, or maybe he's in process, but immigration hasn't given final approval."

"Maybe we will be released from this case this evening. Not that it isn't interesting having Henrik as my partner to find financial information," Jo said, winking at Henrik with a grin.

"Henrik, from all the compliments I hear in the room, you should be a permanent member of our team. Are you interested? I can pay you enough to fly commercial air and stay at a two-star hotel on your next vacation."

"Call me when you need help and don't pay me. I'm always amused by your cases – not that someone has died, rather how you go about figuring out who did it. Maybe if I work for free, you can afford business class on your next flight, no?"

They all laughed at the thought of the Henrik they knew, CEO of Klein Industries, millionaire owner of a private jet, traveling economy, staying at a two-star hotel. Under normal circumstances, their two worlds would never have collided, but since Henrik kidnapped Jill's team from Brussels a couple of years ago to solve the death of his wife, they had become fast friends, with Nathan and Angela helping him with his new venture of a winery close to his home in Stuttgart. He was further cemented in their friendship when he and Marie evolved into a relationship. Despite the distance between Green Bay and Stuttgart, Henrik's travel as a CEO brought him to America and Marie quite frequently.

Jill walked over to Henrik to hug him and said, "We're your weird American friends."

"That you are, and I love your weirdness. I think it makes me creative in my everyday life."

"Alrighty then, Marie, let's continue. Where has he been playing concerts over the past few months? Is he married? Girlfriend?" Jill asked, thinking about how much they didn't know about the victim.

"It seems like his comeback started in Europe and continued to North America. All recitals rather than playing with orchestras, though he was scheduled to play with his first orchestra next month in...Montréal," Marie said, looking at her notes.

"How far was he booked out?" Angela asked.

"He had a one date beyond Montréal, but I think the music world was waiting to see if he came back with talent, but managed to temper his personality. Cutting the strings of a piano is the fastest way to destroy your career from what I read.

"In answer to your question about his personal life, it sounded like he married back home in Russia, but there's been no mention of Mrs. Chernov for a year or so. No divorce or death either. However, I would be the first to admit that my navigating the Russian media and social media is unreliable. I had to translate many posts from Russian to English, and that only works for full words. I can't translate shortcuts like 'lol' for laugh out loud, and he's of the generation that uses a lot of shortcuts. Also, it turns out that Nikita Chernov is a relatively common name, so in my search, I have to make sure that I have the right Nikita."

"Do Russian women take their husband's last name for their own?" Jo asked.

"Yes, most do, but I got the feeling that perhaps ten to twenty percent do not take the husband's name. In this case, I think she did take his name, but it's tough navigating the language difference between English and Russian."

"I can imagine. What else did you find? Parents, siblings, concerns he had about his life, any blocks of time when he didn't post?" Jill asked. "It seems like we have a meritorious, but otherwise average Russian citizen, and fantastic piano player. Certainly, nothing worth killing for so far."

"I thought some people in the classical music world were high-strung, maybe his cutting of the piano strings unstrung someone else, no pun intended," Angela suggested.

What do you know about Russian culture?" Hope asked. "Did he violate some cultural norm?"

"Yikes, you guys have lots of questions," Marie said. "I found just one post of his parents. I looked up his parents separately, and they are what we would call off-Broadway, barely eking out a living performing with other musicians. His mother plays the violin, and his father the domra, which looks to be a cross between a guitar and a Ukulele. I think his parents are a non-issue in this case. He seems to have been an only child, as I couldn't find any records or posts mentioning siblings. In fact, I got the odd feeling he was adopted, but I'm still searching that."

"So perhaps his musical talent didn't come from his parents?"

Jo asked. "I guess that goes to show you how lots of practice overcomes genetics."

"Or if he was adopted, maybe his original parents had musical talent. Certainly, our family has zero musical talent running through it," Angela said, smiling at her mother, who nodded in agreement of some secret musical disaster in the family.

"Not to disparage your work, but he seems like an entirely boring individual, other than wasted musical talent," Jill said.

"I know. When I see this in an employment search, I often find the whole profile has been manufactured, and I recommend a no-hire decision as nobody is this plain, especially at this age."

"So if he is not what he seems, what is he?" Henrik asked as the master of logic. "Any thoughts about why he would lie about citizenship? Is he really the person that won all those awards, or has his person been manufactured from an early age as a cover for something else?"

There was silence in the room as they all thought about Henrik's questions.

"I wonder if some of our questions will be answered by the police or the embassy later?" Jill said. "We'll leave it as a suspicious circumstance on our murder board for now. Jo, were you able to find any financial information on our gentleman?"

"Not without Henrik's help. I couldn't break into the Russian tax system, as much because it made no sense to me, in addition to the language issue. Henrik suggested we trace the deposits of the various piano competition winnings, and so we did," Jo said, smiling at Henrik. "The winnings were deposited to an account in Switzerland that has since closed. So then we looked at where he was staying in Toronto and other cities he'd been playing in to see how the hotel bills were paid, and that traced back to a different Swiss account. Both accounts seemed to be in his name. I couldn't see deposits or anything because they're Swiss accounts. So like Marie, I have a big fat nothing, and I would advise he not be granted a loan like Marie advised he not be hired."

"Sometimes having a big fat nothing is in its own way, a piece of evidence. There is something Mr. Chernov was hiding from the world. The question is, what was it?" Jill pondered for a few minutes before adding Jo's comments to the murder board.

"Angela, what do you have in the way of pictures?"

"I have only one piece of evidence for you. You can see from the time I took this picture; it was at the beginning of Nikita Chernov's recital."

The picture read 11:07 am

"My camera is set to Central Standard Time, and we're in the Eastern Time Zone. Notice the organ pipes," Angela said, zooming in her picture.

"I don't see anything," Marie said, squinting at the image on the wall.

"Exactly! Our archer may have been in place but wasn't aiming the arrow, which is no surprise as it would have lost its shape and puddled by the time it was fired. Unfortunately, from this angle, I can't tell if someone is behind the pipes at this point. I need to go back to the church tomorrow and look at the shadowing to see what I can determine. I'd go back tonight, but natural lighting in the church changes the shadowing, so I'll have to visit tomorrow."

"Henrik and Jack, what does the video footage show you? Anything interesting there? Is there a person walking into the church carrying a cooler? Can you see the suspect on film, and we'll just all continue with our vacation?"

"Whoa, Jill! That's a tall order. No, there's no obvious suspect on the video. First, we plotted what can be seen by cameras inside and outside of the church, and there are huge areas unaccounted for, so I think your killer knew that," Jack said. "We also, mostly Henrik that is, researched what kind of cooler you would need to keep an arrow frozen and in the right shape. What the weight of the arrow might be and things like that."

Jack rose to the front of the room with the two diagrams and added them to Jill's murder board.

"So tell me about the cooler. I hadn't thought of that."

"The hit was relatively close – twenty feet at the most," Henrik began. "It took seconds to fly and hit its target. It would be like throwing an ice cube – it doesn't release drops of water before it hits the target. But, the arrow had to be strong to withstand the tension placed on it by the bowstring. You can make ice stronger by adding impurities to it like sawdust. So hopefully, the crime scene folks will test the victim's clothing to see what residue the melting ice left behind. You can also make ice stronger and colder by using a negative electron charge while it's forming. All of this is to say that if I was serious about the ice arrow, I'd used a good styrofoam cooler – small so the arrow can't bounce around while you walk and I'd take the arrow out shortly before I planned to shoot it. Let me add a few comments about the piano. I don't know if you noticed the piano in my house, but I've played off and on for decades."

Henrik watched the surprise on the faces watching him.

"Where's the piano in your house?" asked Jo, trying to picture it.

"It's in a corner of my living room. It's heavy and bulky so as an engineer, I made a special platform for it that brings the piano away from the wall when I'm playing, and when I'm not, it's closed up behind doors."

"No wonder we didn't notice it," Marie said. "You'll have to play for us the next time we're there."

"Now that I know you like classical music, which is what I play, I will."

Jill's mind was back at Henrik's original comment on being a pianist.

"So, what were you going to tell us about the pianist?"

"The player was playing Beethoven's Sonata in A Flat Major, Opus 110. You all thought it's all played at the same timing, and it is, but I suspect our killer knew his or her victim."

"What?" the single question came flying at him from multiple sources.

"If you are familiar with classical music, you recognize a piece when you hear it played, no?" he asked the group at large.

Heads in the room nodded their agreement with his statement.

"I always know the various compositions of the Nutcracker Suite," Angela said.

"What you may not realize is that while the notes are the same from pianist to pianist, the sounds and the pace are not. The greatest pianists find that special touch with their fingers to make a magical sound. It's why I still play as I'm searching for the perfect sound while I play. In fact, you see pianists talking to themselves while they play, they may be singing the notes in their heads."

"Singing?" Jo asked.

"What about the pace?" Jill asked on the verge of learning something new about their victim.

"Not rock star singing per se, but yeah singing the upcoming notes and hoping to have their fingers strike the same sound as they see and hear in their heads. You have to be a pianist to under-stand. But to your question, Jill. When your pianist played Beethoven's Sonata in A Flat Major, Opus 110, he had his own pace and pressure to strike each key. Most classical music moves to a certain beat, but a well-trained pianist like your victim, would play the notes of the piece at his own pace."

"Therefore, the archer had to be familiar with the pianist's pace and indeed Beethoven's piece to pull the arrow out of the cooler at the right moment to release it from the bow," Jill concluded.

"Exactly."

And there was silence around the table as they all thought of the implications of that piece of news.

CHAPTER 3

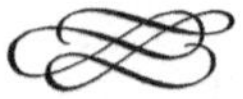

The killer knows his or her victim.

"Maybe we need to get any video surveillance of his prior recitals. I wonder if he plays the same pieces at each recital," Marie said, and looked to Henrik for the answer as their resident piano expert.

He shrugged and said, "I've never played professionally. I don't know what they do. I think we'll have to look at the announcements for prior recitals."

"Good idea! I'll go to work on that. It may be on his Facebook page," Marie said.

"Could someone record how you play a piece, and would the timing be the same each time you played?" Hope asked.

Angela patted her mom's shoulder for having the nerve to ask an excellent question in this roomful of experts.

Heads swiveled toward Henrik for the answer.

Before he could answer, Marie, piped in with, "Nikita Chernov plays Beethoven's Sonata in A Flat Major, Opus 110 in every concert and seems to have a repertoire of four other pieces. His concerts range from two to four pieces according to the announcements."

Her words made the answer to Hope's question all the more relevant.

"I would guess that a concert pianist's timing would have milliseconds differences in how he or she plays. So in answer to your question, Mrs. Weber, yes, the killer could have recorded the piece at a previous concert and practiced taking the arrow out of a cooler with precision."

"Please, call me Hope everyone or Mom will do."

Her comment broke the tension in the room as they all smiled. Nathan thought it was a good time to consider food.

"Well, it sounds like you've nearly solved the case. What does everyone want to do for dinner? I can cook, or we can dine on the hotel's room service, or we could all get some fresh air and walk to a nearby restaurant. There are several excellent restaurants within a quarter of a mile."

"Mom, we'll leave the choice up to you," Jill said. Jill's mother, who lived in Arizona, was also 'Mom', but Jill had always felt comfortable calling Angela's mother, 'Mom'.

"Oh, I'll do what all of you want to do. I'm fine with any of those options."

Angela smiled, knowing her mom wouldn't have been willing to make a choice for the group. She'd been crocheting while they were working and probably wanted to stretch her legs.

"Let's go out, not that we don't enjoy your food, Nathan, but I've been in this suite a little too long," Angela said.

"We have a large group, but it's a week-night. Let me call a few restaurants and see who has seating available now for a party of eight," Nathan said as he went to work looking up telephone numbers.

Jill glanced at the clock, thinking about their upcoming meeting with the police. Now was the time to summarize what her team had for them.

"While Nathan's finding us a place to eat, let me summarize the points of this investigation that we've discovered so far. One, our killer likely knew their victim. Two, our victim is masquerading as an American. Three, we're pursuing video coverage of the other locations the pianist played. Four, he's married. Five his finances are shaky, and last he's a very talented pianist. Did I miss anything?"

"That about sums it up," Jo said, standing up and stretching.

"Okay, we have a reservation. We're eating pub food at a pub down the street. Despite it being a pub, they have high ratings for their food, and I figured the noisy atmosphere would hide any conversation about murder if we all go there," Nathan said, with a smile knowing Jill's team.

"I think you guys should tell us what you learned in your distillery tour," Angela suggested, as they grabbed their coats and purses to leave the hotel suite. "Did you find a whiskey that you fell in love with?"

"I tried a Pumpkin Spice Whisky that I hated, but found a Wicked Citrus Gin that I loved," Jack said.

"How could you not love Pumpkin Spice Whisky?" Jo asked. "You get that flavoring at the coffee shop in the fall."

"Exactly! I felt like I was drinking a coffee drink with a no flavored vodka added. It was the right flavor in the wrong setting with an aftertaste of booze."

"But you liked the Wicked Citrus Gin?" Angela asked. "I like the name, and it sounds refreshing."

"It was. I could see getting into trouble with it, but it was perfectly refreshing."

"And you, Henrik? Do Germans ever drink fruit-flavored alcohol?"

"As you can imagine, beer is our favorite drink, followed by wine. We have lots of summer festivals, and there's a drink served at them – 'Bowle' that is fruit-flavored. It's served in a large bowl, as the name implies. While the punch is usually made with white or sparkling wine, there are fruits or herbs added that have been soaking in gin or vodka for a few days, and that makes them very flavorful."

"We need to experiment with that drink," Marie said. "I think it would be fun to work on the right recipe. How come you've never served it to us when we visited you?"

"Time is always short, and I usually try to impress my friends with wine or beer, not the local village version of punch."

"Make some the next time we're in your neighborhood, Henrik. It sounds like the ladies like the idea of having healthy fruit in their cocktail," Nathan suggested.

"It sounds like the German version of a Bloody Mary," Hope remarked.

"Yes, but instead of it being at breakfast and a vegetable version, this is a fruit version," Marie agreed.

They passed through the doors of the pub and were soon seated after tables were pushed together. Hockey and basketball were on the screens. The Toronto Raptors were playing, and since they won the previous NBA season title, basketball interest increased in Canada. Jill was happy to see the game as the TV sound, in addition to ambient conversation, made sure that her group's conversations wouldn't be overheard. After having their orders taken for drinks, they spent a few minutes perusing the menus. Decisions made and orders given to a waiter, they returned to their distillery discussion.

"Henrik, was there a spirit you enjoyed today?" Angela asked.

"I like wine, and no drink stood out for me, but I did taste one that might appeal to Jill."

"Why?" Jill asked.

"It was painfully sweet. I think it might have made my teeth hurt. I think that's an expression you Americans use."

She laughed and punched him lightly in the arm and said, "Yes, I like my drinks sweet, but even I have limits. What flavor of sweetness was this?"

"Since we're in Canada, it would be maple, of course."

"You'd be wrong then. I wouldn't like it. I hate pancake syrup and adding alcohol to it wouldn't make it any more tolerable."

"I learn something new about you all the time," Henrik nodded at Jill. "I didn't think you had a limit on sweet."

"Oh you're right about that. It's not the sweetness that I don't like about pancake syrup, it's the flavor of maple I don't care for. Besides, I just like butter on my pancakes or waffles, or if I go extreme, some sort of berry mixture in or on them."

"Nathan, you've been quiet. What did you like at the distilleries?" Jo asked.

"I found a flavor I think most of you will like. Hope, I don't know your tastes well enough to guess on this one."

She nodded and he continued, "I had black raspberry gin, and it was the perfect blend of subtle fruit and alcohol. Neither overwhelmed the other. I bought a few bottles so you all can try it later."

"Sounds great," Jill said, happy to see their server likely wouldn't return until their dinner was ready to be served. "Let's share what we'll discuss with the police tonight."

"Why wouldn't you tell them everything you've researched?" Hope asked. "Aren't you compelled by law to do that?"

"Actually, not in the United States. We can't purposely hide evidence like a gun or we would then be an accessory to a crime, but withholding information is done all the time. Canadian law may be different, but again we don't have a smoking gun or, in this case, a melting arrow to hide. I like to be slow in my delivery of information as a way of determining just how smart these people are. It's rather like a chess game, we put forth a detail and then see if they confirm or counter it, to see what our next move is."

"Again, why not feed it all to them in a big feast?" Hope asked again. "Where's the benefit in feeding them snacks instead of Thanksgiving dinner?"

Marie piped in and said, "It seems, in most if not all of our cases so far in whatever country we've been in and despite our collective talents, degrees, and licenses, we are not trustworthy. So the police withhold information from us – like maybe what their crime lab found or what a suspect or witness said. So we have to use information as leverage to get their cooperation. Is that right?"

Angela, Jill, and Jo were nodding their heads in assent.

"We never seem to work with the same law enforcement twice in a row. References from other agencies help, but we have to start at ground zero with each case and prove our worthiness all over again. Mom, do you remember your process for the church funeral meal preparation and serving? You tested each new volunteer to make sure they could follow your instructions and do the work to your specifications. It's sort of the same thing here in our cases; only we're a new group of volunteers for each funeral meal."

Hope nodded her understanding and asked, "So you want to make sure you have all of their information. How will you know when you do?"

"That's a very wise question, Mrs. Weber," Henrik said. "I spend my day observing my employees or business contacts looking for honesty. People's body language tells when they are lying, and you just have to observe them while they talk. In this case, I'll want the police to tell us the pianist is not an American citizen and where his wife is. Surely they know the answer to both."

"I agree, Henrik. I'll also want to know of any evidence collected from his hotel room," Jill said.

"If you don't get that information tonight, what will you do?" Jack asked. He hadn't had much involvement with Jo's work on these murder cases, so he agreed with Hope about telling the police everything they knew.

"Then we'll end the case tomorrow right after the autopsy and resume our vacation," Jill said.

"Why, after the autopsy?" Nathan asked.

"It's the one area of any case that I have absolute faith in my skills as a forensic pathologist. I am the best person to be in that autopsy suite, and if law enforcement comes back later and asks for our assistance, I don't want to have missed the greatest area I could have an impact on. I'll quit the case as soon as I take my protection gown and gloves off."

"You won't do your own lab testing on this case?" Marie asked.

"I spent a little time researching the forensic pathologists here, and they're good. So I think I can direct any testing that needs doing to their lab. Besides, I didn't bring my case with test supplies with me, so I would have had to hustle this afternoon to come up with them. It was easier to verify that the Canadians are good at forensic autopsies.

"In any case, I don't expect any new information to come from the autopsy that we don't already know. We know the cause of death – an arrow through the heart. We know that the arrow melted. There may be a metal point on the front of the arrow. It might have fingerprints on it, but I would have to think they would be smudged. There might be DNA on it, but that may only help once the police find the murderer – a lot of people touched him in the church, in the ambulance, and probably in the hospital, so there's DNA contamination galore."

Jill noticed the waiters bearing down with trays loaded with their meal selections, and quickly changed the topic.

"Hope, are you wowed with the Green Bay Packers being 6-1? I know I didn't expect that at the start of the season with a new coach and the worthless preseason."

Hope took her cue watching the servers unload their trays, "I thought I'd keep a minor eye on the Packers this season, but I wasn't going to let losses upset me, and now I have an entire season to look forward to!"

With the exception of Henrik, everyone at the table was a fan of the football team, and comments about the Packers season carried the conversation until well after the servers left.

Marie showed Henrik the Packer Fans Germany fan group on Twitter. He was amazed to read the German language discussion of the team. He looked up and said, "If I read these comments, I might be able to join your discussion of the team. They play Sunday against the Chiefs, yes?"

Angela gazed upon Henrik as the newly converted in love for her favorite team, clapped her hands, and said, "Very good! You have the schedule correct."

"Why don't you fly in for a game someday? That will seal your devotion," Marie suggested.

Henrik pulled out his phone to look at his calendar and calculated when he would have some free time or might combine it with another business trip to the United States. He might not understand the game, but any time spent with these friends was never wasted.

"I have an appointment in Seattle in early December. I see there's a game on Sunday at noon. I could depart Stuttgart around seven in the morning and arrive at your Green Bay airport about ten. After the game, I'll continue on to Seattle to be there in time for my Monday morning meeting."

"We'll get tickets. Do you want to be outdoors or indoors?" Angela asked.

"I want to be inside the stadium," Henrik said, puzzled by the question.

"The weather could be interesting. It may be snowing or sleeting, or just darn cold. December is always variable inside the stadium," Marie said.

"Are you tough weather-wise, Henrik? You may be sitting outside for three and a half hours at minus six degrees Celsius, or it could be rain or snow. You can get indoor club seats at the stadium to stay comfortable no matter the weather," Jill said.

"I come from tough German stock. We'll sit outdoors. Jill, you and Nathan will come? I could drop you off in California on my way to Seattle."

Jill deferred to Nathan. She hadn't planned on attending the game as it was expensive and time-consuming to fly in for just a game as much as she loved her team. Nathan was a fan because she was a fan, but he didn't follow the team as she did.

Nathan mirrored Henrik by pulling out his calendar and said, "Like you, I have important meetings on Monday. If you could drop us off late Sunday, we could find our way on Friday or Saturday to Green Bay for the game you mention."

Jill was surprised but pleased. Like Angela, she thought that if you sat inside the stadium for a game, you would become a converted fan of the team.

"Hope, will you be joining us?" Henrik asked.

"Oh, no. I'm way past the age of enjoying the game inside the stadium. I'll be much more comfortable in my living room than at the stadium with you people."

"Are you sure? We could get seating inside."

"I'm sure. I would be much more comfortable in my own home."

"Okay, I'll take care of the tickets then. We have seven people, right?' Henrik said.

Everyone else counted in their heads and nodded.

"We'll set a tailgate up at the stadium so you can have the full experience," Angela said. "After you arrive at the airport, you can just take a taxi over to the stadium, and we'll meet you and bring you over to our little party. We could pick you up at the airport, but the traffic is bad around the stadium, so it's easier if you just take a taxi."

"What is a tailgate?"

"It's a party that occurs near a stadium. Food and drinks are placed on your car's tailgate," Marie said. "Check the weather before you leave. If it is minus six, bring a heavy winter coat, gloves, a hat, and snow boots if you have them. Wear snow pants, or have a long coat, or thermals under your pants to stay warm."

A few minutes later, they ran out of advice for Henrik and circled back to their upcoming case with the police.

"Jill, we have comments written on the dry erase boards, are you going to close the doors on those boards before the police arrive?" Marie asked.

"Absolutely! I have our entire case summarized there. I'll either reveal their contents once I see we have cooperation and respect from the police, or I'll show them how great our talent is just before I usher them out the suite door, and we resume our vacation."

"I had no idea, you were such a drama queen," Jack said, admiring Jill's strategy.

"I've given my only acting performances during some of our past cases," Jill replied with a smile.

CHAPTER 4

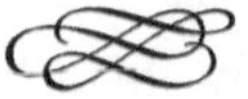

The friends were gathered around their conference table with glasses of Nathan's black raspberry gin in varying degrees of completion when law enforcement officials arrived. Jill had arranged additional chairs and water for their guests, guessing that three would arrive. She was off by two chairs, the Toronto Metropolitan Police was represented by two people, as well as the FBI, and someone from the RCMP. They looked vaguely familiar, but there had been so many people at the scene, she had a feeling that everyone would look familiar.

After introductions were made, Detective-Sargent Hassan asked, "So what do you have for us?

"Why don't we start with what you learned about our victim, Nikita," Jill countered with an earnest smile. It was time to see if they were going to take her team serious as partners.

Hassan looked over at Detective Ireland and nodded and so he began, "As you know, he's a classically trained piano player on tour of Canada and the United States. He was 25 years old and born in Russia."

"I could have found that information on Wikipedia. Tell me what you found in his hotel room," Jill replied.

There was another pause and so she added, "Look, if you don't want our assistance, say so. If you do want it, you need to share information with us. I assume that since the FBI or U.S. Embassy staff isn't here, you've learned he was not an American despite what the program says."

Hassan and Ireland glanced at each other again, and Hassan said, "You're up to date, Dr. Quint. Your embassy failed to find any documents stating that he was an American citizen. However, they decided they wanted to continue to pay for half of your services as they don't like someone lying about their citizenship."

Jill nodded and asked, "So what else did you find about Nikita?"

"He was a temperamental piano player, and it seems that after a particularly bad outburst several years ago, he returned to Russia for about five years. He's doing concerts like the one at the church to regain his reputation."

"Yes, but he only had one more concert lined up beyond Toronto in Montréal. Surely the few he has done recently aren't enough to re-establish his reputation. Do you have any record of his plans beyond Montréal? Where was he going? Did he have an agent? Where is his wife?" Marie asked.

The officers turned to her, seemingly surprised that anyone else was asking questions in the room.

"Wife?" asked Ireland, clearly miffed that he hadn't uncovered that fact about their victim.

"Yes, he married a Russian woman a couple of years ago, but she hasn't been mentioned in the last year or so. However, I couldn't find a death certificate for her, but she seemed to drop off the face of the earth," Marie said.

The two detectives were taking notes.

"Do you know that the killer knew his victim?"

Ireland looked up with his eyebrows going as high up his forehead as his facial muscles would allow.

"How do you know that?" he asked, frustrated about how this

murder investigation seemed to go off the rails. Dammit, this team of Americans had found two critical pieces of information that he and his department hadn't. He felt like he had lost control of the conversation, but maybe he was fooling himself. He'd been a few steps behind the doctor and her team from the start.

Ireland looked at Hassan for a moment before glancing back at the women sitting comfortably around the conference table, awaiting his next move. A little late, he discovered why they had such a reputation from his peers down south in the United States.

"While we're the professionals, we seem to be several steps behind you with this investigation. Tell us why you say that victim knew his killer."

Jill looked over to Henrik as it was his knowledge that had prompted the conclusion.

He gave a slight nod to her and said, "I've studied and played the piano for decades. Our killer would have had to hear our piano player play Beethoven's Opus 110 several times to get the timing perfect for releasing the arrow. Every classically trained piano player plays that piece marching to a beat in their head. So you couldn't just listen to a recording and assume that the dramatic chord was played at the same second in the music."

"Could our killer have just visited the city of Nikita's last performance? I think that was Detroit," Ireland asked.

"Maybe, but you wouldn't get the timing right by just listening to one performance. Besides, Marie pulled up the announcements of his recitals, and he did play this Beethoven composition in every city. So the killer could have heard him play several times in several different cities, or heard him practice."

"We'll check to see if there is video surveillance of the audience at each of the venues. How many were there before Toronto?" asked the detective.

Marie looked down at her notes and said, "Five."

Jill looked around the room, trying to assess whether she and her team had earned respect, grudging or not, of the Canadian law enforcement officers. She decided to give them the benefit of the doubt, and so she stood up to open the dry erase board doors lining the dining room of their suite.

There was silence in the room as the detectives stood up one by one to read what was written on the boards, taking pictures with their cameras. Nathan poured another round of drinks while they waited for the officers to break the silence.

"I understand why your references spoke so highly of you and your team," Hassan said. "We will share with you what we have. Detective Ireland, please share our findings from our investigation."

About time, thought Jill.

"Our medical examiner searched our victim's body for any evidence of a murder weapon," Ireland started.

"Wait, I thought the autopsy was scheduled for tomorrow. Was that rescheduled without notification to me?"

"No, Dr. Quint. We needed to work on the weapon, and so we asked if the medical examiner could search for and remove any artifact of the arrow without doing the full autopsy. I understand Dr. Thornton used magnifying glasses and removed the arrow without otherwise disturbing the body in less than a minute. The autopsy is still scheduled for tomorrow morning."

Jill nodded, that was a reasonable effort on the part of Dr. Thornton to attempt to remove and document any evidence of the arrow.

"The arrow was sent to our lab for analysis. The DNA analysis will take weeks to get the results and likely will only be useful when we go to trial to convict our suspect."

"Fingerprints?"

"None. One of the detectives in our division is a bowhunter. He said that archers rarely touch the tip. When you pick up an arrow, you hold it in the middle and connect the end to the string of the bow, so it's no surprise, that there were no fingerprints."

"Did your hunter speculate on how you could make an ice

arrow and keep it cold?" Henrik asked. He had some ideas, but wanted to hear what the police said.

"Our lab gave us a variety of suggestions, but the most feasible suggestion is dry ice in a styrofoam cooler. It would keep the arrow perfectly frozen for up to twenty-four hours. If the removal of the arrow occurred quickly, there would be little fog arising from the container for spectators to notice. The arrow would be so cold from the dry ice that it wouldn't start to melt by the time it was fired from the bow. We'll need to talk to someone at the university to determine exactly how much time the arrow would have had before the ambient temperature affected its shape. We concluded that the archer practiced their technique prior to this shot. It could not have been a spontaneous moment of anger that caused the murderer to kill Mr. Chernov."

"He or she must have scouted the church to understand where they could take the shot out of view of the public," said Angela. "Every church has a different layout of the organ pipes, piano, and sanctuary. In fact, I bet the piano was moved into place for the recital as it would be in the way for services. I would say our killer had visited the church during another recital to see where the placement of the piano was. This concert series is offered every Friday for several months each year, so it would be easy to stop by the church on another Friday to see the positioning."

"From what you've said about the murder scene, this murder feels like it happened in cold-blooded passion. I know that sounds like an oxymoron, but to time Nikita's death with the music feels passionate, while the way the killer did it feels well-planned. They had to scout this church, the organ pipes, the sanctuary. They had to get the timing right on the particular piece, and they had to make and perfect a lethal ice arrow. It feels like a very grand passion behind your victim's death," Nathan said.

Nathan rarely said anything about their cases and especially to law enforcement, but she could tell he was intrigued by how their pianist died and the creative thought that went into the murder scene.

Nathan's words gave everyone pause while they thought about their killer.

"So was it a man or a woman?" Hope asked. She wanted to put a vague face on their killer, and she would start with their gender.

"Could have been either. Without knowing the mechanics of the frozen arrow, we have to assume it could be anyone. Angela has a picture of the partially melted arrow, and it looks to be about two feet long and perhaps at most, an inch in diameter or roughly the weight and size of an icicle. The torque to pull the bowstring back to send the arrow the short distance would suggest that anyone of moderate strength could have been the killer," Jill said.

"True," agreed Detective Ireland. "We have not been able to rule out either gender, but oddly this feels female to me."

"Perhaps it's a professional hit given the planning that went into it," Marie suggested. "The killer had to know the location, the interior of the church, the position of the piano, the selections the piano player would play, the timing of the music, the design and refrigeration of the arrow. There is an awful lot of preparation that went into this murder. Perhaps more than I've ever seen on any of our previous cases."

Jill thought the circumstances around the murder reminded her of the case in which Henrik's wife was murdered. It had been well planned and sophisticated, but now was not the time to remind him of that tragedy, and it had no bearing on this case other than the fact it was a woman who murdered her.

"How about the arrow tip?" Jack asked. "Any idea where you can buy such a thing? I checked a website while you were all talking and arrow tips are readily available."

"Yes, I should have added that our crime lab researched the tip and found lots of sources for it, assuming it was even purchased in Canada. It could have easily been brought across the border from the U.S. so researching the location where it was purchased from is thought to be fruitless at this point," said Ireland.

Several people nodded at that comment, and Jill saw a few hidden yawns by her friends around the table. It was emotionally exhausting watching a murder happen, and the adrenaline rush created by the flight or fight response drained everyone. She thought they were probably done with the information exchange and so it was time to call quits it for the evening.

She looked over to Hassan and asked, "Detective-Sargent Hassan, I think we're done unless you have any other information. I'll see you or perhaps Detective Ireland at the autopsy tomorrow morning."

The meeting broke up, and the hotel suite's living room emptied, with visitors departing and the residents of the room heading for their bedrooms and some well-deserved rest.

Jill was crawling into bed next to Nathan, and he asked, "That was a long day; but everyone seems to be handling it well. I hope no one has dreams about the murder. Do you think everyone is doing okay?"

"Well, they're not dead, so on that scale, everyone is doing splendidly. Everyone that witnessed the murder had to have had an adrenaline rush with the event, but looking around our table, I'd say that the camaraderie of our friendship mitigated any lasting effects of that rush. Wouldn't you agree?"

"I would. You and our circle of friends that we developed over the past couple of years have enriched my life, and built it to withstand the rigors of life. I do love you, Jill."

Jill leaned in to kiss him, murmuring, "Love you to the moon and back."

CHAPTER 5

"Are you researching already?" Jill asked of Marie as she looked in the refrigerator for breakfast options. It was always better in her estimation to have something in your stomach while experiencing the scents of the autopsy suite.

"Yeah, I'm on the search for Nikita's wife. I can't believe she has just disappeared off the face of the earth with no notice. I'm also trying to do a timeline of our victim's life when he returned to Russia. What did he do all day? If he wasn't earning income from performances, then how did he cover his living expenses? It's a challenge trying to break through Russian websites. First, there the language problem, then there's the issue of disinformation. I'm going to use this search to write a protocol for other searches at work as we occasionally get applicants from foreign countries. So my protocol will deal with translation into English and how to tell when you need to translate, as well as the legitimacy of the website."

Marie's day job was creating dossiers for candidates seeking employment in her large Wisconsin company.

"Glad one of our investigations helps your day job!"

"One of my co-workers mentioned that I return to work energized by our cases, and she was right. I have learned new ways to collect information on our cases. There's also the feeling of being grateful to be alive after being chased through a cave by the Sicilian mafia," Marie said, referring to their last case.

"There is that feeling of exhilaration; at the same time, it makes my imagination wonder how bad the person may be behind this murder, and how might they represent a danger to us? Is it a single person or some Russian organization? We've faced all of these options in the past."

"I'm planning to continue searching today, but unless someone in our group speaks Russian, I doubt there is much for them to do."

"Yes, I agree with you. Our group should continue with the plan to visit Niagara Falls, and then we may leave on schedule for Montréal tomorrow as there may be nothing more for us to do that requires our presence in Toronto. I need to leave for the autopsy, but see if you can herd everyone toward having fun in my absence today, would you?"

"I will. I'm having fun with this search, so I may or may not join them depending on where I am, but certainly, the remainder should enjoy the Falls. I was there seven years ago, so unless that natural wonder has changed, I won't be missing anything more than the camaraderie of our friends and whatever wineries or distilleries, they find along the way."

"Sounds like a plan. Say hi to Henrik for me. See you later," Jill said, leaving the suite for the walk over to the University. The police had offered to send a car for her, but when she found that her hotel was near the subway, she offered to have them meet her at the Yorkdale Station, which was much closer to where the autopsy would take place.

There was a light mist in the air, enough to require the hood of her jacket to cover her head, but not enough to bring out the umbrella from her purse. Looking at the sky and the weather report, she knew the weather would clear by the time her friends left for the Falls. She ducked into the subway and was quickly onboard her train for the Yorkdale Station. She glanced at her fellow commuters, wondering if any of them were connected to this case and then smiled to herself at her fanciful imagination. One station before Yorkdale, she texted the number she'd been given the night before for her ride, letting them know she'd soon be there. She kindly received a text in return with a picture of the car that would be awaiting her and directions to exit directly to Yorkdale Road. Apparently, there was a mall at the subway stop that generated a lot of traffic, but it was closed this early in the morning.

Jill exited the subway station as instructed and found Detective Ireland leaning against the car from the picture. It was a nondescript sedan car which pleased Jill. There was nothing worse than getting into the back seat of a police cruiser when you weren't a criminal.

"Good morning, Detective. Any new evidence overnight?" Jill asked in her usual abrupt manner.

"We haven't been able to do anything with following up with the previous venues that our victim played at as they haven't opened yet. We can gather additional video locations around the church, but we're not sure how to narrow hours of video into looking for our killer."

"I can help with, or rather my colleague Henrik Klein can help with that. He's developed a fantastic facial recognition software used by many law enforcement agencies around the world. I have a copy on my laptop, but he's the inventor, and so is a much better resource than I am."

"The trouble is, we haven't a clue as to what our killer looks like."

"True, but maybe we could limit the time we collect the video and see if we find anyone in common. We know the killer had to visit on a Friday as they would want to see the arrangement of the piano. They would need to be in the church before the recital started or just after it finished to make sure they had an accurate view of where the target would sit. They also needed to get behind the organ pipes and know of a quick exit out of the church, so given those parameters, we could collect tape on perhaps no more than twenty hours of footage. Then we could put a software program to work identifying who appears in multiple videos. We might finalize our list down to twenty or thirty people. I say that number as there are probably some people who regularly attend the free noon recitals. Still, we should be able to identify them and eliminate most of them as you have their names as witnesses in the audience. If you were in the audience, you couldn't have also fired the arrow, right?"

The detective was visioning the killer learning the specifics of where their target would sit, and Dr. Quint's suggestion sounded like a good one if they had some kind of computer software to aid them.

As he pulled into a model looking multi-story glass building, Jill looked across the field to a hospital designated by its large blue H on the top. She'd bet that the coroner's office was a little too close for some of the patients in that hospital. It was a reminder that we all had to die sometime, but one didn't want that reminder necessarily when they were sick in the hospital.

"This is an impressive looking facility, and it looks relatively new."

"It's about six or seven years old and a massive upgrade of the old facilities we had. It does important work for the Province of Ontario."

Jill nodded as they entered the building. She followed the detective to the autopsy area and the female detective from the previous day was on hand to take Jill into the dressing room.

"How are you, Detective Kim?" Jill asked.

"Good. I'll show you where you can put your clothes and where you can find scrubs."

The detective was a woman of few words, or perhaps she was

not a morning person. A few minutes later, Jill was attired in clothes similar to ones she'd worn for hundreds of autopsies. The detective directed her into the suite, where the victim lay on the cold metal table covered by a sheet at the moment. She was introduced to Dr. Thornton, the medical examiner on the case. After a brief discussion of Jill's credentials and training, they got to work.

"I've received some early lab work from Mr. Chernov taken at the hospital and shortly upon arrival here last night. His ATP is beyond normal guidelines, as are a few other tests. He had the early stages of organ failure occurring, which is highly unusual for someone so young. I'm looking forward to examining his liver and kidneys to see if any physical damage matches the lab values," Dr. Thornton said.

"Are you saying that if he wasn't killed by an ice arrow, that he would've died soon?" asked Detective Ireland.

"Yes. Dr. Quint, you can review the results over on that terminal," Dr. Thornton said, pointing to a computer behind Jill.

She walked over to the computer and moved the mouse. She scrolled through a variety of lab reports.

"This is interesting. Nikita is from Russia, and I do not know about the safety of drinking water and other environmental toxins that reside in that country. However, these lab results indicate that he was suffering from the symptoms while on tour as a pianist. That suggests to me that he continued to have exposure to whatever substance was causing organ failure outside of Russia."

Without warning, everyone that had been standing close to Mr. Chernov's body took several steps back from the metal table upon which his body was resting. Jill asked the question that everyone was wondering about in the room.

"Did you run a Geiger counter over Mr. Chernov's remains when they arrived here?"

"Yes, it's part of a routine protocol. Besides, he has a full head of hair."

Jill nodded, "Yes, on the surface, I don't see acute radiation poisoning."

Detective Ireland was standing by the door to the autopsy suite and asked, "Is it safe to be in here?" as he didn't understand what conclusion the two pathologists were discussing.

Jill looked at Dr. Thornton, both of them sorting through their training and experience to determine if the body in front of them might present some danger to them.

"You can't test for alpha particles with the Geiger counter, so he could have been exposed to polonium, but again he has a full head of hair, so that likely rules that out. Still, I'd like to have a radioactive shield to be in this room." Jill said, looking around for an apron that x-ray techs typically wear.

They exited the room and checked with experts on how they should handle potential radiation exposure. After consultation and a physical check by a radiation physicist, Mr. Chernov was determined not to be at risk to anyone in the autopsy suite. If he had consumed polonium, his own body would shield them from radioactivity. The two pathologists unnerved by the scare of radiation proceeded to do one of the fastest autopsies in their professional careers. Rather than Jill observing Dr. Thornton, they agreed she would do half of it with Dr. Thornton supervising for purposes of future legal proceedings.

In record time, Mr. Chernov's body was ready to return to the cooler. So far, they had been unable to locate any family and referred the disposal of his remains to the Russian Consulate General in Toronto.

"So what did you learn from this autopsy?" asked Detective Ireland.

Jill waited for Dr. Thornton to speak as he was the official here.

"The lab values prompted us to focus on your victim's liver and kidneys. You could call those organs 'human body filters'. So if someone is exposed to any kind of toxin, foreign substance, or poison, typically those substances show up and damage those organs. Does that make sense?"

The detectives, nodded and so he continued.

"We were alerted to problems by the lab values. We confirmed organ damage by physically examining those organs. We collected further samples to send to the lab to determine the source of this damage. We may not have answers for three weeks as it takes time to run through all the possible sources of toxicity and identify the source. It's even a little more difficult as our victim has spent a lot of time in Russia, and therefore we may be looking for a toxin that is rarely seen in Canadian labs."

Jill thought that Dr. Thornton described the situation very well. He spoke in a language easily understood by non-pathologists, and he gave a timeline of when they could expect more information. Jill had one thought to add to the explanation.

"Once the lab identifies the toxin, it likely won't help your investigation."

She noticed the confusion on the detectives' faces, so she continued.

"Whether the toxin can be found in Russia, Canada, or the United States, it doesn't much limit your list of suspects. If the toxic agent turns out to be polonium, then you are assured that Russia is behind this murder as it is impossible to get that agent in North America. However, Russia is a big country with a lot of people, and so this does not limit the suspect list by much. You would still have millions of Russians as suspects. What the autopsy tells us is that there was a slow effort to kill Mr. Chernov that someone lost patience with and so took care of him in the dramatic gesture of shooting him through the heart with an ice arrow."

The detectives nodded their understanding, and Dr. Thornton excused himself to do further documentation on the case. Jill headed into the dressing room to change back into her street clothes. A few minutes later, they were walking out to the detective's car. On the way, Detective Ireland had explained Jill's suggested process for looking at the video to identify a suspect.

Detective Sargent Hassan passed a message to the detectives requesting they bring Dr. Quint with them to the Detective's Operation Unit for more conversation. He had been backing up his Chief that morning for a press conference about the murder. It was a sensational case as it occurred in front of the public during a dramatic moment of the music with a weapon that no one had seen before. There would be strong media interest in the case for a few weeks, and if it went unsolved, the interest would still be there as a cold case in the future of Canada.

When Jill heard the request, she wanted to comply, but first, she needed to check-in with her friends to see what their plans were for the day. She stepped away from the detective and called Nathan.

"Are you awake?" Jill asked, knowing that Nathan wasn't a morning person.

"I'm surrounded by you morning people, and somehow it bothered my sleeping conscience that I might be missing out on something by sleeping the morning away, so yes, I'm awake. In fact, I've already had two cups of coffee. What's up? Did you learn anything from the autopsy?"

"We did. Someone has been trying to kill the pianist the slow way, and concluded it was a good idea to put him out of his misery with the ice arrow."

"That's terrible. Not only was his young life cut short, but I assume from your comments, that he was miserable the last few days or weeks, because of something someone was doing. On a happier topic, Henrik has arranged a van to take us to Niagara Falls. Should we stop by and retrieve you from the detectives?"

"As much as I love spending time with you and our friends, I've been invited into the Detective Division of the Toronto Metropolitan Police. I'll take that over Niagara Falls any day."

Nathan chuckled on the other end of the phone knowing that Jill's comment was exactly right for her.

"Alrighty then, we'll see you tonight at dinner. I'd say that we're going to have a better day seeing a natural wonder, but I know the Detective's Division is your idea of a natural wonder. Do you need us to drop anything off to you on our way out of town?"

"As a matter of fact, I'd love for you to drop off my laptop and Marie. We talked before the rest of you got out of bed this morning. She's already seen Niagara Falls and is enjoying the search on our victim. So if you could drop her off as well with her laptop, maybe we can make some progress on this case."

"You two are peas in a pod. You like the thrill of the search. I'll pass the information on to Marie and see you soon."

Jill texted the address of where the detectives were taking her, and then let the detectives know that her laptop and Marie Simon would be dropped off to meet them for work on the case. Jill watched their faces as she delivered that news and could tell they were not thrilled by having another member of her team enter the workspace of their realm. Oh well, she was getting used to constantly proving herself to law enforcement. They would soon find out that she and her team were the best.

CHAPTER 6

Marie and Jill were seated inside a cubicle in the Detectives Division, waiting for someone to arrive from the Metropolitan Police's Property and Video Evidence management office. They were expected to come with video surveillance from around the church for the past three Fridays in addition to the day of Mr. Chernov's murder. Jill needed someone smarter than her to piece together all of the footage, so the software package would look through all of the hours of footage for matches. She wondered how fast or slow the software would search the video. Would it be twenty minutes or eight hours?

It would be a real test of the software to see if it could locate a suspect. So far, the killer had covered their tracks well and very detailed oriented. In many ways, it was a perfect crime. For the killer, they got rid of someone they wanted dead in the most dramatic and public way possible, and then they vanished without a trace. That took some skill. So when they looked at the video, will the killer have disguised their features enough to fake out an artificial intelligence software program? Maybe they would get lucky and find the killer was arrogant and made no effort to hide. Meanwhile, Marie was working with Detective Kim in the search for the victim's wife. Marie thought she had come across a picture of the woman, and if she could find that picture again, she would save it for Jill to run it through the software program.

Detective Ireland obtained their victim's credit card receipts for the past several weeks since he'd been trying to re-establish his reputation as a concert pianist. They had new data to run down. Just tracking his movements should lead them to his killer as they had to have crossed paths several times before his death. At the moment, the detective was mapping the locations of his movements based on the credit card receipts.

Jill paused a moment to discuss a theory with the two detectives, "So we've been working on the assumption that there is just one killer here rather than a team. We should probably discuss that assumption."

Detective Ireland responded, "We know a single hand fired the arrow from the bow, but I suppose you're correct that we don't know if it took a team to help the killer get to that point inside the church."

"I can't think of any evidence we have that would allow us to draw a conclusion one way or the other," Detective Kim said.

"But...it feels like a single person for some reason," Jill said. "Perhaps because Mr. Chernov's murder feels so passionate. A terrorist cell might feel passionate about a target, but in my experience, this doesn't feel like a team."

Jill thought she saw Detective Kim roll her eyes out of the corner of her eye. She silently sighed. Just when she felt she gained respect from the detectives, Jill now questioned if she had been invited to the station out of proper Canadian courtesy. She would file that away in her head and track whether they were sharing all of their information with her.

She looked up to see a person approaching carrying a laptop. This must be their property and video surveillance person. She briefly crossed her fingers that Henrik's software would work in its usual perfect form.

They spent a few minutes discussing how to connect the two laptops given the data-rich nature of the video. Once they worked that out, the facial recognition software went to work. It began spitting out faces, names, and videotape locations where the faces were seen on the tape.

"This is rather scary software. It's so powerful," said Constable Thompson, who Jill guessed was the leader of his police division. "I've heard rumors of this software at police meetings, but never saw a demonstration of it."

"Once we see what it kicks out as far as accuracy and relevancy, we may be your biggest supporters for the purchase of the software. I suspect it is not cheap," said Detective-Sargent Hassan as he joined them at the cubicle to watch.

"Sir," acknowledged Kim and Ireland, a nod of respect to their supervisor as they were too entranced by Jill's program to stand up.

Good, thought Jill. Finally, they were impressed by something she brought to the table. Though to be fair, it was Henrik's software they were impressed with and not her creation of it. Instead, they knew they were fortunate to potentially witness its assistance with a case.

In the end, the program kicked out more people then Jill had initially guessed. There was a core set of listeners for the free Friday concert series. There was also a popular coffee shop close to the church, and the street cameras recorded them walking one way empty-handed, and again with a coffee cup in their hands. These people were put on a secondary list to research if the others didn't pan out.

"So we have an initial group of twelve people to do more work on, and another twenty-three likely related to the coffee shop, that may require more work in the future," Hassan summarized. "I

also have to say I'm impressed with your friend Mr. Klein's software. This could be quite a tool."

The other detectives nodded, impressed by their potential
ability to come up with a suspect out of a seemingly endless
universe.

Marie looked up from her laptop and said, "I found her. Let's
see if we can identify who she is and if she's in any of the
surveillance."

"Who did you find?" asked Thompson, not sure what this
other woman from the United States was doing to contribute to
his colleague's case.

"The women labeled as our victim's wife. I don't believe we
met, Constable," Marie said, standing up to shake hands. "I'm
Marie Simon, I do online searches for Jill to get a social picture of
anyone involved in one of our cases. I also have a day job, and I do
the same thing to form a 'hire/don't hire' picture of any candidate.
In my searching yesterday, I came upon mention of a spouse, and
then she disappeared from the world. Our victim returned to
Russia five years ago and seemed to marry, and then about two to
three years ago, all online mention of her disappeared. Here's her
picture," Marie said, turning her laptop around for everyone to
see.

It was a distant picture, and they could see that Marie had used
translation software to learn what the Russian words accompa-
nying the picture meant.

Anna Chernov was at an International Women's Day party.

"I looked that up, and it's like Mother's Day in the US and
Canada except you don't have to be a mother. It's as important
and as flower giving as Mother's Day according to a Russian site,"
Marie added.

"Could this be his sister?"

"Good question. Let me look up Russian names. Maybe
women don't take husband names, or maybe brothers and sisters

have different last names," Marie suggested before going to search for answers to her own questions.

"We have quite a Russian population in Toronto, and I'll bet we have someone on the force who is Russian speaking and knows something of the culture," Thompson suggested.

Hassan nodded and send a text to his assistant to see if he could locate such a resource.

Within a minute, he had word back from his assistant that an officer from Division 53, which included one of the Russian neighborhoods, was on her way into the detective division to assist. She was expected there within ten minutes.

"Thanks, Thompson, that was an excellent suggestion. We have a Russian-speaking officer on her way here with an ETA of ten minutes. Perhaps she can educate us on all things Russian. If nothing more, we'll at least understand the naming process in the Russian community, so we know what we're looking at."

"We're going to start running down the names we gained from the software. I have a question for you or Mr. Klein. If our suspect disguised him or herself, is there a way to change the setting on the software, so it looks for a lower facial match to capture any disguise?" Ireland asked.

"I don't know the answer to that question, so I'll text Henrik," Jill took a moment to do just that. "I do know that it's harder than you think to disguise certain features. Fake beards, sunglasses, and hats don't work to disguise your features. Generally, you need LED lights near your chin or forehead like in a hat brim to effectively disguise your features."

Jill felt her phone vibrate and said, "Henrik says there is a way to reduce the accuracy of facial recognition and therefore catch a larger swath of people, but he doesn't advise we make that change as in his estimation the data becomes worthless at a certain point. I'm to text him when we're ready to go to less accuracy, and he'll walk me through the change."

They were just starting their research of the twelve people when officer Yelena Orloff arrived in the division. Detective-Sargent Hassan gave her a quick briefing on the case and who the players were seated in the cubicle. She stood at attention and listened, took a look at Anna Chernov's picture, and then provided an explanation.

"She is likely his wife rather than his sister. Women commonly take their husband's name now in Russia."

"Is it unusual that there are so few pictures of her?" Marie asked. "I'm surprised there are not multiples of them together as a couple like you find all over the world."

"It depends, in Russia, the State controls the media and so they can make you disappear socially or physically. My guess is that someone has doctored that website to eliminate her."

Jill's screen lit up indicating that the search was completed.

"There's no match for her picture with anyone in any of our videos."

"Russian Intelligence may have prevented her departure from Russia. Also, it is extremely rare that a wife would kill a spouse. The divorce rate is over fifty percent, and so it's a lot less messy to get rid of a spouse legally," Orloff said.

"Let me ask you a cultural question. Based on what you heard here, do you think the wife could be our killer?" Jill asked of Orloff.

"I'm not a detective, but if your question is, would a Russian wife follow her husband to North America to kill him? The answer would be 'no', just like you don't hear of many American or Canadian spouses killing each other abroad. In Russia's history, alcohol was involved in about eighty percent of all murders, and as you can imagine some of those murders have taken place between spouses. However, alcohol consumption has dramatically declined in Russia, and so has the homicide rate. Sir, do you have any further questions?" Orloff asked of Hassan once she finished her explanation to Jill.

"No. Thank you, Officer Orloff, and I'll be sure to note your helpfulness to us with your commander."

Orloff saluted and left the detective division.

"Okay then, it's on to our twelve suspects. Since we have names, it may be as fast for Marie to investigate these people as for the police to do so. Let's start with the first name," Jill said.

Jill caught a look that passed between the Canadian officers that suggested she overstepped her bounds, but she didn't care. She'd gotten them to this point in the investigation with the twelve potential suspects and Marie's identification of the wife.

Ireland got a text and said, "Dr. Thornton has a quick identification of the agent affecting Mr. Chernov. It was arsenic. It far exceeded the level found in people around the world, so he says it couldn't have come from groundwater or other sources. He was definitely being slowly poisoned. Glad that we didn't have radiation exposure."

"You know what they say about poison – it's a woman's first choice for a murder. I wonder if said female got impatient with the process and decided to take care of him in a more absolute way," Jill said.

Marie said, "Suspect number one is an American teacher on vacation in Toronto. She teaches band for middle school students in South Dakota. She was here for ten days and attended two concerts. I would guess you can take her off the list of suspects."

Detective Ireland looked surprised that Marie had found the information so fast on the first potential suspect on their list. He was impressed that she was faster than any employee in his cop shop. He decided to let her continue reviewing their suspect list. Then his division would step in once she couldn't eliminate someone. Each time she pulled someone up to look at, Jill found the corresponding video. They would all watch the video looking for something, but they were already a third of the way through the list, and no one was walking funny or looking suspicious on the tape.

Marie was halfway through the list when she said, "Okay, this person doesn't exist."

Jill saw detectives Kim and Ireland readjust their shoulder harnesses as if to say, 'little lady, don't worry your head, we'll find the information you're too slow to locate.'

With that bit of body language, Jill blatantly rolled her eyes and gave the detectives the raised eyebrow and said, "Go for it, Detectives."

Thirty minutes later, they admitted defeat, unable to find any information on the person in the photo.

"Is it a male or female?" asked Detective Kim, voicing Jill's uncertainty with the image.

"I have no idea," replied Marie. "Jill, does the software indicate what it thinks the gender is of the person in the photo?"

"Good question. Let me look."

There was silence in the room as she hit a few keys to look at different aspects of the software.

"On the photos it matched, it indicates gender. For this suspect, there's a sixty percent chance that it's a male according to artificial intelligence. Glad to see the computer is as confused as we are. So gentlemen, what are our next steps?"

"About once every five years, I run into a candidate with no presence on the Internet. It's extremely rare, but it has happened. Just because we can't get any information on the person in the video doesn't necessarily mean that he or she is our killer. I'm just making that statement on past experience researching people," Marie advised.

"At this point, we move the person to the top of our suspect list. Still, we haven't finished searching the entire list, so let's make sure we do that first. I don't want to be distracted by someone without an identity while the real killer gets away," Detective Ireland said.

The room was silent as they all went back to their sources to look for information about people on the list. As far as Jill was concerned, Marie was the best person in the room at investigating people. So while everybody else concentrated on researching the candidates, Jill studied the videos of their unidentified suspect looking for clues as to which gender the person was. She tried zooming in looking for facial hair, but the quality of the video didn't allow her to do that. She studied the various video frames looking for shapeliness that would suggest female. She also watched the person's gait, knowing that male and female hips moved differently. In the end, she decided she agreed with the computer software program as there was nothing inherently feminine about the unknown suspect.

Jill then moved on to texting Nathan to see how the tour was going at Niagara Falls. Looking at her watch, their van should've arrived there by now.

He texted back, 'We just arrived, have a fifteen-minute wait for the boat to take us behind the Falls. It looks cold.'

She texted back, 'Maybe you can find another distillery in the area and warm yourselves up with some whiskey after the tour, lol.'

'That's a brilliant idea. I looked, and there are three nearby. Will try them out and let you know if we find any winners. How's your day going?'

'Okay. The police are waffling on whether Marie and I are helpful. So just my usual irritation with law enforcement. Love you.'

He texted a final salutation, and she tuned back into the room. She glanced over at Marie's laptop and noticed she had crossed most of the other suspects off her list, with brief notes about her decision. She was obviously doubling down with her search on the final picture that their software came up with. Jill moved closer to Marie to watch her fingers create magic with the keyboard. Still, at this moment, there was no magic to be found as she couldn't locate any information about the final picture. Marie leaned back and focused her attention on the room.

"Did you find anything on the eleventh picture?" Marie asked the three detectives in the room.

"No. So we have two unidentified suspects on our list of twelve. Ms. Simon, you say that you do background searches for people all day in your day job. What are the odds of two of twelve individuals having blank histories in your experience?" Hassan said.

"Infinitesimal. I can't recall a single search of a candidate list that I've done in the past decade with two candidates with empty backgrounds. Granted, the people I'm searching for are looking for jobs. Therefore, they have usually put something out there, while these two people were just trying to listen to music and not gain employment. So the circumstances are different."

"How about if I get some more video for you folks from additional streets around the church so you can see where these two unidentified people came from?" offered Constable Thompson into the silence.

"Jill, can you tell how the software came up with their names?" Marie asked.

Jill spent some time looking around the database then said, "There's a different source for different pictures. Some are American or Canadian driver licenses, while others are passport pictures. We have two people we can't seem to learn anything about. One, we don't know the person's name or even gender. The other we have a name and no additional information. The source of the name only suspect came from a passport that was used to enter Canada from the United States. The country of issue for the passport was Estonia. Is Estonia filled with classical music fans?"

Detective Ireland looked up from his computer and said, "We have an Estonian Embassy in Ottawa. I'll give them a call and see what we can find about Voldemar Tamm."

"Do you have the Canadian equivalent of the CIA?" Jill asked.

Detective-Sargent Hassan gave Jill a pained look.

"Yeah, I know it sounds fanciful, but you have someone in your country, in your city who you can't identify. Isn't that unusual?"

"We have the Canadian Security Intelligence Service, but we're going to have to do a lot more groundwork before I put a call into them. Let's get more video footage. Constable, how soon can you have additional footage for us to analyze?"

Constable Thompson looked at his watch and his phone and estimated, "Thirty minutes, sir."

"Let's take a break for lunch. Dr. Quint and Ms. Simon, can we host you in our cafeteria?"

Jill looked at Marie, who shrugged, "Sure, why not?"

CHAPTER 7

When they regathered after lunch, Constable Thompson had new footage for them to review. Jill put the software to work and sat back while it did its thing. She guessed it would take about fifteen minutes to give them a result. She was wrong. The software was much quicker as it was trying to match their two unknown suspects to anyone in the additional footage. She had a result in under two minutes.

Constable Thompson said to Hassan, "Sir, if I request the software in my budget next year, I presume I will have your backing? This might be the most amazing tool I've seen in my career with the police."

"I agree, Constable, and you'll have my support. Let us hope that it doesn't break the budget, and we have a realistic chance of obtaining it. I don't suppose your Mr. Klein has a discount rate for police departments."

"I have no idea what kind of arrangements or costs are associated with this system. I believe I have the one free copy in the world," Jill replied.

"We're going to put the word out in the law enforcement community that if they hire you, not only do they get an amazing team and a forensic pathologist, but you come with very valuable software."

"That will work," Jill said with a laugh. "Thanks for the recommendation. Do you have a map of downtown Toronto? I'm a visual person, and I would like to plot our suspect's movements as that may tell us something."

"We have a big city map in our briefing room. We could go over there and discuss the movements of these two individuals," Detective Ireland said.

They walked over to another room on the same floor and stood to study the map. Their street video expert, Constable Thompson, walked them through the paths that the two men took in the vicinity of the church.

"I'm not sure this gives us any additional information. We can't see where the men came from or even if they got out of a taxi just beyond the view of the lens of the camera. It feels like our focus is too narrow," Detective Kim said. "None of our video footage shows either of these two suspects carrying the smoking gun, or in this case the ice arrow or an archery bow."

"Those are good points, detective. Maybe we need to go back and look at video footage for up to twenty-four hours before Mr. Chernov's death. We need to see someone carrying a fairly large bag entering the church, and then leaving without it. We need to return to the church and look for hiding places for such a bag. Where they could stash the ice arrow in a cooler until they needed it. I'd also like to verify that between the interior cameras of the church and exterior cameras on the street, that we have all church entrances covered. That would give me greater faith in our methodology," Jill said.

"Maybe we can also see the crime scene pictures taken by your staff," Marie suggested.

"That's a good idea, Marie. Even though the murder took place in front of my eyes just over twenty-four hours ago, I'm losing the fine details of the church as I remember the scene. Let's visit the church first, then look at pictures."

Detectives Ireland and Kim accompanied them to the church, which still had crime scene tape draped around it with a notice that it was closed until further notice by the Toronto Metropolitan Police. There was a lone officer seated just inside the doors with a clipboard, booties, and rubber gloves for official staff to wear inside the church. A short time later, they were appropriately registered and suited up, and they proceeded toward the sanctuary. Yesterday, Jill had not had the opportunity to look behind the organ pipes, and she was anxious to see the view of their killer. They had been admonished not to touch anything despite wearing the gloves.

Jill and Marie took a seat in the pew they had sat on the previous day so that the movie could begin in their heads of the murder. Once Jill had refreshed that scene in her head with the physical view of the pew in front of her, she got up and approached the sanctuary.

The piano bench was still turned over from where the pianist had tumbled backward after being hit. Jill squatted at the piano, trying to understand the trajectory of the arrow from where the pianist would have sat. Then she approached the organ pipes to see if there was any evidence of the arrow's journey through the pipes. She could see no discernible difference to suggest to her through which two pipes the arrow had moved. It was silent inside the church as though the building itself was giving hushed reverence to the previous day's event. There was the occasional creak or groan in the nearly 200-year-old church.

Jill stood in the sanctuary, moving her eyes between the organ pipes and the piano. "Somehow, I didn't remember that these pipes were as far as they are from the piano. I also didn't realize the pipes were as high as they are. He was shot at a downward angle, and so our archer would've had to practice that. This looks about five feet down and a distance of twenty feet that suggests to me more expertise than I expected from our archer."

"Yes, crime scene technicians estimated one and a half meters down by six meters distant," said Ireland looking at something on his phone. It must be a report from the crime scene staff.

Jill was rusty at doing the calculations in her head between feet and meters, but it sounded close to her numbers.

Jill saw lots of space between the bottom of the organ pipe points and the floor. Someone wearing black would not show up in the light behind the pipes.

"Can we go up to that level?" Jill asked, pointing at the pipes.

"Yes, our crime scene techs went up there, so I'm sure there's are stairs. Let's start wandering around to see what we can find," replied the detective.

Jill had watched a few videos on pipe organs the previous night to understand how they worked and how they were configured. It looked like a profoundly difficult musical instrument to master. Different churches had different pipe organs, and their size and configuration seemed to be more about the church than a standard design for organs. Some of the largest pipe organs had over eight-thousand pipes with some pipes weighing upwards of one-thousand pounds. Somewhere in the church was a massive air handling system that moved air in and out of the pipes to make a sound. She thought back to the murder and the symbolism of an arrow flying out of the massive pipes of the church organ to the puny pianist playing the tiny baby grand piano in comparison.

Jill was taking notes as they walked through the church and drawing a sketch of the interior with the position of the piano, the organ pipes, and doorways. As yet, she didn't know where all the doorways led, but she would have it all mapped out by the end of her tour. Eventually, they found the pathway to the level of the pipes the archer was located in when he or she released the ice arrow. It was narrow, and Jill mimicked pulling back the string of a bow.

"There sure isn't a lot of room in here. Our killer would need a fairly narrow bow with a powerful string so they would only have to pull it back a few inches as that is all the room they have here. I also think because of the narrowness of the space, our killer would have had to stand. What did the crime scene techs conclude?" Jill asked the two detectives.

Detective Kim looked through her notes on her phone and said, "They believe the arrow was fired from a height of 1.67 meters given the entry wound. So basically, someone my height. An arrow would be fired from eye level, and since I'm about 1.7 m tall, I'm about the size of our killer, give or take a high forehead."

Jill would have performed the weapon calculations as part of the autopsy, but this was an unusual case in that the weapon melted after it was used, which would've made any calculations about the angle of the weapon tricky and beyond her scope as a forensic pathologist.

She looked around the space for any additional information, but nothing caught her attention. She touched one of the pipes to see if it was movable. The pipe was fastened to the ceiling tightly and really had little give to be moved aside.

"So how did our killer arrive at this spot? Did they come in the front door? That seems unlikely as you would've thought that someone from the church staff would ask why someone was walking toward the pipes rather than having a seat in the pew," Marie said.

"I agree with you. We need to look at all the entrances to see how you can get to this point without being stopped by a random church person. I think as long as you didn't move and were clothed entirely in black, our archer could have stood behind the pipes for several hours."

Jill and Marie began their own walking tour of the exterior church doors. Along the way, they paid attention to any interior cameras protecting the church. After walking around the exterior and the interior of the church, they speculated on a path that their archer might have taken.

"Here's my theory. There's a regiment of Scottish guards attached to this church, including a museum in the basement. It's possible to walk in the front door, go down to the basement to visit the museum and continue on to the back stairs, which would then allow you access to the walkway where our archer stood. I think we need to go back and look at the video from when the church opened yesterday and see if anyone entered carrying a package. When we looked at the video today, I don't believe we went that far back. I'm done here, are you detectives ready to return to your base?" Jill asked.

Detectives Kim and Ireland had been conducting their own inspection of the church while Jill and Marie did their walk around. They had separately reached the same conclusion that the two Americans had. In fact, they had a conversation with the Lt. Colonel of the Scottish Regiment to understand the museum and their role in the church. They were a reserve militia unit that had proudly served in World War I and II, and more recently, in Afghanistan. The two detectives learned a little bit more about their city in their everyday work as detectives. The museum was only open to the public for a few hours on Wednesdays and Thursdays, so there would've been no foot traffic in the museum area on a Friday.

"We agree with you on how our archer entered the church. What's your theory for how they exited the church? Somehow I don't see our suspect exiting down the front stairs after they've murdered a pianist," Kim asked.

Jill cracked a small smile and repeated the detective's words, "We agree with you. There are two exit doors to the street behind the church, and if I had just murdered someone in front of a crowd, that's how I would've left the church."

The detectives had contacted Constable Thompson with the task of collecting all videos for the day of the murder. He had some of that ready to go for when they returned to the detectives' division. The church was a little slower to respond as their staff was in temporary disarray with the closure of the church. He thought he would have the interior video once they were done looking at the public closed-circuit cameras footage.

It was approaching late afternoon, and Jill thought that other than looking at the new video, they had no more work today to do on the case. She texted Nathan to find out where the rest of their friends were and what their plan was for the remainder of the day. Maybe she and Marie could join them for some fun after this day of concentrated research.

'Where are you guys and what's your plan for the rest of the day?'

'We'll be back at the hotel in about an hour. I'm cooking tonight, and desserts are coming from the hotel. Will you be joining us?'

'Yes, in fact, we might arrive at the same time.

"Productive day?'

'Just sold another customer on Henrik's software.'

'I'll let him know. Is the killer in custody?'

'No.' Jill responded with a sad emoji.

'You can tell us all about it with a glass of wine.'

Jill texted back several wine emojis and relayed the evening's plans to Marie.

"I feel like we've been sitting all day. I'd love to get a quick three-mile run in on the treadmill before dinner."

"Go for it. I doubt you'll have any competition. Certainly, this is not my time in the day to exercise, and I'm looking forward to that glass of wine from Nathan. Maybe I can get a workout in tomorrow morning."

They settled into their seats in the detective division, and Constable Thompson presented them with another flash drive of video for Henrik's software system to analyze. This time Jill asked it to look for people carrying bags or backpacks. She'd never done this kind of search before, so she was curious as to what would turn up. Would it identify women with small cross-body purses or people carrying umbrellas, neither of which she was interested in?

This search took a little longer than the previous one, she guessed because, in many ways, faces were easier to match then random bags. In addition, as this was the video from the streets around the church, there were a lot more pedestrians passing by that had no relation to the church or the case. When the software indicated it was done with the search, she was dismayed to see just under two-hundred hits of people carrying bags. She started viewing the video frames picked up by the software while everyone else leaned over her shoulders looking at the laptop screen.

"I think we're going to have to examine each frame," she said. "I can't think of a way to tell the software to be more exclusive in its search with the potential that we miss an important frame of the video. Besides, I think we can quickly eliminate the small purses and bags, not of a size to contain a frozen arrow and bow."

"Can you make a copy of the report so we can work backward from the end and get through this list of frames faster?" asked the Constable.

"Let me see," Jill said and then click a few buttons and asked for an email address.

She, Marie, and Ireland went to work reviewing the front half of the list, while Kim and Thompson reviewed the end of the list backward. They met in the middle half an hour later, each with a much smaller list of about five frames of video. Jill ran that collection through the software again, looking for names to identify the people carrying bags large enough to conceal the murder weapon.

"Bingo! The software found our friend Voldemar Tamm carrying a large enough bag to conceal our frozen arrow and bow. Furthermore, he appears to be wearing all black clothing, which would be necessary to stay hidden behind the organ pipes," Jill said.

The detectives were rather amazed and breathless at the speed that the software worked to help them identify a suspect. Never in their careers had they seen such a tool to help them solve a crime. In the age of security cameras everywhere, this was a valuable tool that the department needed to purchase. They didn't like working with the American and her civilian friends, but they couldn't deny that the two of them had made the most significant contributions to the case.

Detective-Sargent Hassan rejoined them and asked, "I need an update for the Chief. Do you have any new information?"

"Well, sir," Ireland said, "It's early yet, but we just might have identified our murderer. Have you heard anything from the Estonian Embassy?"

"No, it's a slow process going through diplomatic channels. Tell me about our suspect. What have you got?"

"We have no concrete evidence yet, but our video footage suggests that our shooter is Estonian citizen Voldemar Tamm. He's seen entering the church carrying a bag that could contain our styrofoam chest holding the frozen arrow as well as a bow. He is seen visiting the church several times. He is seen entering the church on the day of the murder, but not exiting. On his last visit to the church, he is dressed in all black, which any suspect would have to be to hide behind the organ pipes. An extensive research of his history shows no history. Except for his entrance into Canada with his Estonian passport, there seems to be no other evidence of his existence. I realize this is all circumstantial evidence, but we're going to work on putting him behind the bow that fired the arrow that killed Mr. Chernov," Detective Ireland explained.

"That's a lot of circumstantial evidence, but you're right it's not enough to get the court to issue an arrest warrant."

"Do you think it's enough to block him from exiting the country?" Jill asked completely unfamiliar with Canadian criminal justice law.

"I think we have enough suspicious circumstances that we could hold him within this country and hold him within the police station for twenty-four hours. I'd rather just keep him under surveillance and prevent him from leaving our jurisdiction. Do you know where he is?" Hassan surmised.

"No, that's the trouble - we have no information on him. He may have left the country already," Ireland said.

"Well, at least I'm going to contact our border patrol so that if we have the opportunity, we can stop him from leaving the country. We'll also check with them to see if they have a record that he already left."

"Hopefully, he doesn't have a fake passport and therefore uses a different name to leave Canada with a different passport. I think Marie and I have done what we could to assist the Canadian government today. We're going to return to our hotel, and knowing the two of us, will do some more research tonight or tomorrow, but otherwise I don't know how we can contribute to your case, do you?"

The three detectives would love to see the American doctor go and not return to assist them with the case. They recognized that their feelings were irrational, and the good doctor had done nothing to antagonize them. They just didn't like strangers in their domain, and to be fair, she and her teammate made the enormous contributions to the case so far. They really hoped their department would be able to buy the software that she had demonstrated with such agility.

"Can I say on behalf of the Toronto Metropolitan Police that you've been very helpful to this case? We've never worked with civilians before or even non-Canadians, but thanks to you and your magnificent software our best leads have come from your efforts. If you learn anything from any of your efforts over the next couple of days, please contact us," Detective-Sargent Hassan said, handing Jill the business cards of the three detectives and the Constable. "Now, may we give you a ride back to your hotel?"

Jill looked at Marie, who nodded in agreement, both of them thinking it was likely the fastest way back to the hotel. If the rest of the gang wasn't there yet, Jill could get a head start on her wine, while Marie could get that work out in.

"Yes, I suspect that would be the fastest way to return to our hotel. Detectives and Constable, it's been a pleasure meeting you, and I wish you luck in gaining cooperation from the Estonian Embassy," Jill said, standing up and shaking hands with Marie imitating her movements. Soon they were at the curb, and a patrol car arrived to take them back to the hotel.

CHAPTER 8

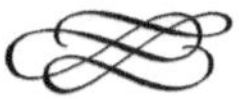

They beat their friends back to the hotel, and soon, Jill was in the suite living room stretched out on the sofa with a glass of wine thinking while listening to the rhythmic patter of Marie's feet on the second-floor balcony tread-mill. She was staring at the ceiling, wondering if she'd thought of every angle possible for this case. She thought about her autopsy case at home and the tools it contained to help her solve cases. She had a worksheet built around autopsy findings. The purpose of the worksheet was to cause her to think about sources of the various pathological findings. She thought about the autopsy that morning, and had they exploited it for all the possible informa-tion it contained? Is there more she could do research-wise with the discovery of the arsenic poisoning?

Then she remembered something they had not discussed at all – his personal effects. What did the police find in his hotel room? Was he living with someone? What kind of hotel was it? Who paid for it? The other piece of information she was missing was why he was listed as an American citizen. Did he supply the misinforma-tion, or was it an error on the part of the church? The more she thought about it, there are some really strange miscellaneous bits of information about their victim Mr. Chernov. Surely the police knew the answers to her questions as they would have been a routine part of their investigation. She got up and wrote the questions on their whiteboards, then sat back down.

She was still staring at the ceiling when she heard the door unlock, and suddenly there was the noise of six people having multiple conversations amongst each other. The tone was one of happiness. Apparently, they'd had a great day visiting Niagara Falls, and wherever they went after their Maid of the Mist ride.

"Hey friends, it sounds like you had a great day at Niagara Falls, and whatever you did after the boat ride. Marie is showering after running, while I'm staring at the ceiling looking for inspiration and enjoying my glass of wine."

Nathan sat down next to her while everybody else found somewhere to sit.

"So, where did you go after Niagara?" Jill asked Hope.

"Well, dear, we went to a brewery and had excellent burgers and beer. Your Mr. Nathan here wants to cook us dinner, but I'm still full from lunch. Did you solve the case?"

"We found them a suspect, but it's really up to them to locate the guy and arrest him," Jill said. "We don't know where he is or even if he's left this country considering his passport says he's from Estonia. I must say it's very suspect – European passports are easily faked by companies in Thailand, which is the forgery capital of the world for passports."

"So you caught them on camera with the bow and arrow?" asked Jo relaxing into Jack's side.

"No, it's not that simple. We collected lots of video footage from the streets around the church and got some bow and arrow expertise from the police. There is someone on a camera at the right time carrying a bag that is the right shape to contain a styrofoam cooler and a fold-up bow. We visited the church and figured out the best way in and out of the building. Then with Henrik's magic software, we identified that person on video as Voldemar Tamm, an Estonian who entered Canada from the U.S. about a week before the murder. When we left the police station, they still hadn't heard back from the Estonian Embassy in Ottawa. There's nothing more we can do at this point."

"I could do a search of the guy's financial records," Jo offered.

"I could run him through my master database back in Stuttgart to see where his face has been seen before in the world? It will take all night, but the computer is doing the work, not I," Henrik said.

"Since I suspect that Voldemar Tamm is not his real name, go ahead and look Jo, but don't expect to find much. It would be better to examine his financial records after Henrik does his run. So I guess I'm saying there's a little bit more we can do to help the Toronto Metropolitan Police find the suspect."

Jill handed Henrik the laptop in front of her that contained Voldemar Tamm's picture so he could have someone in Germany do a computer run. It was nearing 11 o'clock at night in Germany, so Henrik gave a brief thought to who was likely awake at that hour to do this computer search for him. He didn't want to wake anybody up, so he texted someone he thought was awake and waited for a response. A minute later, he punched the send button on the email containing the assignment and handed Jill's laptop back to her.

"Are you sure you don't want to become a permanent member of my team? The offer is still there - you'll get two-star hotels, economy seating on planes, death threats, and perhaps one-thousand dollars on each case. Doesn't that sound more appealing than being a technology CEO with a private plane?" Jill said, razzing Henrik.

"I've got a counter offer for you. Why don't I pay you ten thousand dollars on each case as you seem to sell my software? I'll give you the title of marketing manager."

"No, thanks. I have enough titles already – vintner, forensic pathologist, private investigator, and friend to everyone in this room."

Jill received a round of applause when she named the last title.

"So what are we doing tomorrow? It's our last day here before we move on to the Province of Québec," Jack asked.

"We may have a few hours of work in the morning, depending on what Henrik's mega-computer comes up with. I have one thing I'd like to do, and that's to visit a cemetery where my grandmother and a favorite great-aunt and uncle are buried. My grandmother died when I was four or five, so I have no memories of her. My favorite great aunt and uncle, I spent many holidays and vacations with here in Toronto and at their cottage on Rice Lake, which is perhaps an hour north of here. I have some artificial flowers that I would like to leave at both gravesites. All three relatives have been dead for decades, so it's a matter of respect that I pay a visit. I don't know where the graves are in the cemetery or what kind of markers they have. I understand there are 160,000 people buried in the cemetery, so it may take me a while to find them. I have their plot numbers, but like I said, it's a big place. "

Marie joined them freshly showered and glowing from her run on the treadmill and said, "Why don't we go now? We have a few hours of daylight left, and that should be enough to find what you're looking for. Having been cooped up inside for most of the day, I wouldn't mind an outdoor walk even if it is a cemetery."

Jill looked at Nathan and said, "How does that fit in with your plans? I believe you're planning on making dinner? Did you have a timeline on that?"

"Actually, that sounds like perfect timing. I'll stay here and cook and whoever wants to go with you can visit a cemetery. Mom Weber, if you would like to stay here and be my assistant, you're about the only person among this group that I would trust to share the kitchen with," Nathan said with a grin but also knowing that the older woman didn't need to be walking in a cemetery after the long day they had at Niagara Falls.

"I would be happy to assist you in the kitchen, dear. I'll let the young ones go off and ramble through the cemetery. Besides, the wind is picking up, and it's already been a windy day," Hope said.

The others gave some thought as to whether they wanted to visit a cemetery. Henrik wanted to return to his suite and get a little work done, so he declined, but everyone else was on board to visit Jill's relatives in this large Toronto cemetery. Jill took a look at the weather on her phone, and indeed Hope was correct that the wind had picked up considerably since they returned to the hotel. The forecast said that there would be wind gusts of over 30 mph. She appreciated that her weather app stayed in American measurements as the Canadian equivalent sounded closed to hurricane speed.

They needed to get a move on with darkness coming in two hours. After gathering up coats and scarves for protection against the wind, the five friends were split into two taxis on their way to the entrance of the cemetery. Jill had diagrammed the cemetery on paper so they would all have their own map to help her look for the grave markers. At this time of day, the cemetery office wasn't open, and so they would have no customer service help to find what they were looking for.

The taxis drop them off at the front gates, which were closed to cars at this hour. Fortunately, the pedestrian gates were open. Before they arrived at the cemetery, they passed through several ethnic neighborhoods, evidenced by Spanish or Italian restaurants and storefronts.

Once they walked inside and looked at the section map, Jack asked, "How large is this cemetery? I can't see where it ends."

"It sits on two-hundred acres, and there are twelve miles of roads inside the cemetery. Think about it, there are far more people buried here, then are alive in the city of Green Bay, Wisconsin. That takes a lot of land, and there are still people being buried here, so it hasn't run out of room yet. It's about one-hundred-fifty years old. It's about a third the size of Arlington

National Cemetery, so as big as it is, it's not likely the biggest cemetery you've ever been in," Angela said.

They all looked at her, sharing so many facts about the cemetery.

"Well, I looked it up before we came here. It sounded large, so I needed to put it in perspective of the only other large cemetery I visited."

"You weren't kidding when you said we would get lots of fresh air here. Between the distance, we have to walk and these wind gusts, this cemetery will blow all of the indoor air out of my body," Marie said.

"Can I just say, it's a little creepy here with the wind blowing and the trees rustling?" Jo said. "There's a lot of ambient noise here from the wind that stirs my imagination."

"To quote Sonny and Cher, I've got you babe. I'll protect you from the ghosts," Jack said, putting his arm around her.

Jill pointed to a gently sloping hill in front of them and said, "We need to head that way. My great aunt and her husband are in a section perhaps half a mile on the right."

Knowing that they didn't have endless daylight, they hustled up the hill to see nothing but an unending cemetery in front of them. The wind gust frequency picked up, and the fall leaves blew around them at a high rate.

The road flattened out, and Jill looked for a cemetery marker designating what section was before them.

She could see the marker up ahead and said, "This is the section where my great aunt and uncle are buried. Start looking for marker number 1321. There are about three-thousand graves in this section, so it may take us a while."

They spread out in the section, each trying to find the numbering sequence. Their search was hampered by not knowing if there was a simple grave marker or a large monument head-stone. They all ducked when they heard a branch crack in the wind and drop to the ground nearby.

"Whoa, the wind is wild," Jack yelled over the wind. "They're going to have a real mess on their hands tomorrow. I can't imagine trying to keep two-hundred acres in pristine condition for whatever funerals are planned."

"Found it!" called Marie. They all ended their search and rushed over to where Marie appeared to be looking at the ground.

"Frederick and Anne Kinsley," Jill read aloud. "Yep, you're looking at my favorite Great Aunt and Uncle. Let's take a moment and see if we can clear this gravemarker a bit."

They all kneeled around the two-foot by one-foot marker to clear the dirt and grass that had overgrown it. Jill, Jo, and Marie used ballpoint pens and nail files to clear the stone while Angela took pictures of the stone and its place in the cemetery. Jack could only watch as he had no tools. In short order, Jill laid her artificial floral arrangements on each side of her relative's names.

She stood up and said, "That's as clean as we can get it. I wish I'd thought to bring tools, but I thought it would be in better condition than this. We need to keep moving, as we still need to find my grandmother. It might take a while as she's at the other end of the cemetery. I think we have to cross a public thorough-fare to reach it."

They followed the map, which contained switchback roads as the path to the exit. Jill sighed and made an apology to the residents resting in her path and cut directly to the first exit. Indeed they had to cross a street that was busy enough to warrant a bus stop. Fortunately, on a late Sunday afternoon, it was relatively quiet. All around them, the wind continued to gust, and trees groaned as dusk began to arrive.

Jill said, "We have about forty-five minutes of daylight left, and then we can exit this cemetery to the west and hail a taxi on Eglinton Ave. We're looking for Section 32, which will be on the right side after perhaps a five-minute walk."

"I hate to tell you this, Jill, but it's getting creepier for me. The daylight is dimming, and there are a lot of dead people around us.

The wind is making an otherwise quiet place into a noisy cacophony of sound. I keep looking up to see if we should duck."

"Just turn off your imagination for another half an hour, and we'll be out of here. There's no one else here, and we're perfectly safe, it's just the atmosphere is getting to you."

"Is this the section your grandmother is buried in?" Angela asked, pointing to a marker.

Jill checked her paper and nodded yes, and then she spied something in the distance and pointed, "Look at that black cat over there. It probably belongs in one of those neighborhood houses behind that fence over there. Do you think it's trying to tell us where my grandmother is resting for all eternity?"

Jo replied, "I think that's a beautiful idea, and we should start close to it first in our search. When was she buried?"

"1966 and with my mother's family in California first and then later, Arizona, and my uncle's family down under in Australia, I suspect she hasn't had any visitors in decades. It's all rather sad."

"How old was she when she died?" Angela asked.

"Young, I think - only sixty. It was a car accident that both my parents and she were in. She later died at the hospital of a heart attack. Both my parents were critically injured and unable to attend her funeral. I think my mom's been here once to visit."

"There are a lot of grave markers in this area; there's a number on several of them. What number we looking for?" Jack asked, trying to read all of the memorial stones as they pass them in the search for Jill's grandmother.

"423."

They knew they we're close based on the numbers, but many of the grave markers were overgrown and unreadable.

"What's the name on this marker?" Marie asked.

"Ireland, just like the country and the detective. Her maiden name was Packer."

"You were destined to be a Green Bay Packers fan," Angela said solemnly.

"I was. It took me a while to find my heritage in football, but I found it now and haven't let go."

"This might be it," Jack said, kneeling down to pull the grass away from the marker and clear the leaves away.

Jill sighed and said, "Another family grave marker in poor shape. Let's get our crude tools out and start digging." She had a bouquet of artificial red roses that she laid next to the marker as they began clearing it. Again Angela captured the setting and their efforts to clean on camera. When they were finished, Jill left the flowers in a little vase and stood up for her final review of her grandmother's grave.

The wind had been blowing and branches cracking the entire time they had been in the cemetery. It was very atmospheric and powered everyone's imagination.

"All I need is some rattling chains to make a run for the exit. By the way, which way is it from here?" Jo asked.

Jill pointed to the cemetery road and said, "We'll return to that road and take a right, and the exit shouldn't be far away."

They heard another branch crack, and they all instinctively put their hands over their heads, thinking from the sound it was close by.

Marie yelled over the wind, "There aren't going to be any trees standing by tomorrow if this keeps up."

Jill yelled, "Duck behind those large memorials. That wasn't a cracking tree; it was a gunshot."

CHAPTER 9

Marie, Angela, and Jill took cover behind one memorial while Jack and Jo were behind the other. "What should we do?"

Jill had taken her cell phone out of her purse along with a business card.

"I'm calling Detective Ireland. Angela, can you use your camera lens to get a fix on our shooter? Be careful - try to keep your head below this memorial and just raise your camera and try to look at the screen."

After five rings, her call connected, "Detective Ireland, this is Dr. Jill Quint, and I'm in Prosperity Cemetery with four of my friends. We are being shot at and have taken cover. We need help immediately!"

There were a bunch of holes in Jill's explanation, but in his short acquaintance with the American, he knew she wasn't prone to drama or exaggeration.

"I'm on my way, and I'll call additional resources. That's a big cemetery, tell me where you are, and you can tell me later what you're doing there."

"I'm visiting my grandmother's grave. She's in section thirty-two, near the western edge of the cemetery after Rogers street but before Eglinton."

"I'm going to put you on hold while I talk to dispatch and get additional cars on the scene. Hold on."

While she waited for the detective to come back on the call, she asked Angela, "Have you spotted our shooter or indeed any human out there in the cemetery?"

"I think I've seen someone moving over near that Greek Goddess Headstone, but my distance eyesight isn't very good. Marie, can you take a look?"

Angela and Marie switched positions, and Marie studied the view from Angela's telephoto lens after looking quickly around, not wanting to be a target.

"Are you sure that wasn't another branch cracking?" asked Jo tucked behind another memorial in the same row as Jill.

"Yes. A cracking branch doesn't cause concrete dust or leave a mark of a headstone," Jill said, pointing to a damaged headstone.

"Oh," Jo said, the humor and hope leaving her eyes.

They could hear sirens in the distance and could only hope they were heading their way.

Then they heard another crack, and Angela's camera flew off the ledge of the headstone it was sitting on.

Detective Ireland came back on the line to Jill, "Give me a status, is anyone injured?"

"Not yet. A second shot was just fired, and it knocked Angela's phone off the headstone. We were trying to use the telephoto lens to spot our shooter."

"Units are on their way, you should be able to hear their sirens. ETA to the western edge is one minute."

"The gates are locked at this hour; how will they get in?"

"We have bolt cutters in our cars. I'm still five minutes away."

"I think we should start moving from headstone to headstone toward the western exit. We're sitting ducks here."

"Okay. Be careful."

Duh, thought Jill. No, they were going to stand up and walk tall toward the exit.

"Guys, let's get a move on. We're sitting ducks here. I don't have any advice other than to zigzag and stay low."

Jill made the first move dashing to another headstone. She saw the path in front of her with a number of tall memorials that they could take cover behind. She briefly glanced behind her and saw that her friends were following in her footsteps. She didn't see anyone moving behind her that was the potential shooter. Then with gratitude, she saw flashing red and blue lights heading their way obviously on the inside of the cemetery. If she and her friends could just stay unharmed for another sixty seconds, she was convinced that they would make it out alive.

She heard another crack of a gun, not a tree branch breaking, and then Jo cried out behind her, and she stopped ready to render aid to her friend.

"What's wrong, where were you hit?"

"The bullet didn't hit me. It hit the concrete above my head, and now I have concrete dust mixed with my contact lenses. I won't be able to see until I wash my eyes out. Jack, you're going to have to guide me."

The four friends looked worried, but then heaved a sigh of relief when they heard the roar of a car, the ear-piercing sound of the siren, and blue and red lights that were almost within touching distance. The officers got out of their squad car but took cover behind the door, knowing that they were responding to a call of shots fired. They left the lights flashing, but turned off the siren.

Over the PA speaker, they heard, "Jill Quint and friends, turn on the flashlight feature of your cell phone and briefly flash it in our direction so that we know where you are."

There were a few seconds of delay as those that didn't have their cell phone in their hand fumbled for it, and then five lights flashed toward the police car.

That was immediately followed by a bright light focused on where the gunman was thought to be.

The PA again came on, and they heard, "This is the Toronto Metropolitan Police, put down your weapon and come out with your hands up."

Jill looked around her area to assure herself the gunman was not closing in. All she could see was a darkening void in front of her. Marie and Angela crouched against the memorial stones, while Jack and Jo were sitting against another headstone with her hands covering her eyes.

Silence reigned in the cemetery except for two additional cars arriving, another patrol vehicle, and what looked like Detective Ireland's car. The officer and detective approached the first patrol vehicle maintaining protection of the car. A second light was aimed at the cemetery, which apparently was an infrared light.

"Okay, Jill Quint, you can come out of hiding as there are no additional heat sources in the vicinity other than you and your friends."

Detective Ireland approached, and Jill called out, "Does anyone have contact solution, eye drops, or clean water? One of my friends has been blinded by the headstone dust created by a bullet. We need to wash her eyes out."

One of the officers asked, "Do we need to call an ambulance for you?"

He heard a chorus of 'no' coming from the group of Americans.

She saw the patrol officer approach the trunk and pull out a first aid kit that contained eyewash. He gave it to Jack along with gauze to help Jo rinse her eyes. In a short time, Jill could see that Jack and Jo were making progress with her vision and so she turned her attention to Detective Ireland.

"Thanks for getting here so quickly. I thought Canada was safe why would anyone shoot at us in a cemetery? We didn't even see the gunman to know if it was a male or female."

"You're safe now. Slow down, and let's start at the beginning. Tell me what happened. When did you arrive at the cemetery? You said you were visiting your grandmother's grave. I had no idea you had Canadian roots."

"I was here to visit two graves. I have a great aunt and uncle buried in section eleven, and we stopped to visit them first. My grandmother passed in 1966, and she is in this section. Each grave marker was overgrown with grass, and so it took a while to clear it off, and I left a bouquet of artificial flowers at each site. By the way, her last name is Ireland also, so perhaps we're related."

"Did you see anyone else in the cemetery? It's large, and you must have had at least a mile walk between the two gravesites."

Jill looked at her watch and said, "We've been here about ninety minutes. Once Marie and I got back to our hotel, our friends arrived back from Niagara Falls. I knew we had about two hours of daylight left, and so it seemed a perfect amount of time to come to visit these two graves. But the weather was wild, and then we were shot at. Walking through the cemetery with high wind, we heard a lot of branches cracking, and my friends thought it was just another branch at first when they heard the gunshot, but I knew better. We quickly scampered behind some tall memorials, and I called you."

Jill saw the other patrol vehicle drive toward the other entrance of the cemetery. She didn't think they would find anything as the gunman had had time to go over one of the residential fences that lined the walls of the cemetery, but it wouldn't hurt to look.

"How many total gunshots did you hear?"

Jill paused and replayed the tape in her head to make sure she had the right answer, and then she said, "Three. I managed to find the bullet that knocked Angela's camera off the headstone."

She reached into her coat pocket and pulled out a bullet using the sleeve of her shirt to keep her fingerprints off of it. The detective pulled a plastic bag out of his coat and opened it for her to drop the bullet into.

"That's one of three."

"We'll get a metal detector out here to hopefully locate the other two bullets and maybe even the shell casings. Who knew you were coming here tonight or rather this afternoon?"

"Nathan, Henrik, and Hope remained at the hotel, so they knew our destination. We got to the hotel lobby and asked the doorman to get us two taxis since there were five of us to bring us to the cemetery. And that's it, the decision to come here was quite spontaneous. It was on my list of things to do while visiting Toronto, but I hadn't scheduled it to take place this afternoon."

Detective Ireland was beginning to understand how the American doctor's mind worked through a problem, and so he asked, "So what are your theories about the shooting?"

They were interrupted when the patrol car returned and called the detective over to it. There was a conversation, and then the patrol car left heading toward Rogers street.

The detective returned and said, "They've searched the entire cemetery, and other than the five of you, there are no live humans or even recently alive humans in the cemetery. They've gone back to resume their patrol, and the crime scene crew is on its way here. So back to my question, what are your theories, Dr. Quint?"

Jill thought through her answer for a few moments and then said, "I don't believe you have a killer on the loose in Toronto randomly shooting cemetery visitors. I believe we were the targets, and I have to believe we were the targets because of our connection to this case. What I don't know is how anyone found out that my team and I were working on this case. No one has made such an announcement. So I think I was watched at the church either at the time of the murder or when we visited earlier today and then I was followed back to the hotel and back out again. So my conclusion is there is more than one person involved in this murder."

Detective Ireland nodded, "My mind was working through the problem after I got your call. I immediately concluded that you were the target. I will admit that when I contacted resources in the United States, I was forewarned that you had a magnetic attraction for killers. Once our killer heard you were on the case, they would do their best to put you six feet under as your American cop shows say."

Jill gave him a pained look for his honest assessment then added, "I think we also have to conclude that either your department has a leak, or our killer has additional people on his team including our gunman. By the way, how hard is it to get a gun in Canada? I know you have hunting here, but what kind of rules do you have if I want to fly a gun into Canada or cross over from the U.S. with a gun? Can I just hide it in the car, and you won't notice at the border?"

Now it was the detective's turn to look pained. Before he could answer, Jo, interrupted their conversation.

"I've got the concrete dust mostly out of my eyes now, and I'd like to return to the hotel so I can rinse them more. My contacts are toast, but they were disposable, and I have a back-up pair, but I think my eyes are so irritated that I'll be wearing my regular glasses for a while. Detective, can you call a taxi in here so I can get home? I guess you'll want to interview me at some point, but Jill would tell you that I'm pretty oblivious to the world at large, and so you won't gain anything by interviewing me."

"This is true, Detective. She is not a good witness. Can you help with getting her a ride back to the hotel?" Jill asked.

He noted the crime scene van arriving and decided that since he now had more staff around, he could afford to have the patrol car take the woman and her partner back to the hotel. Jo and Jack were soon on their way, and he needed to pause to speak with the crime scene crew, handing them the bullet that Jill had recovered.

Jill took the time to call Nathan.

"I think we might be late for dinner."

"What happened?" Nathan asked, his voice filled with tension.

"After we found my grandmother's grave, someone began firing shots at us. I'm here with the crime scene staff and Detective Ireland. Jack and Jo are on their way back to you at the hotel. She was our only injury in the event because she got concrete dust in her eyes from a bullet striking a headstone near her face," Jill rushed her explanation, somehow feeling the anxiety rising from Nathan on the other side of the phone call.

"How many shots were fired? Jo is the only one injured?"

"We believe three shots were fired, but it's hard to say for sure because the weather is wild. During our entire visit to the cemetery, trees have been swaying in the high winds with occasional branches cracking. It's a similar sound to gunfire. Jo is the only one injured, and she was able to wash her eyes out with supplies from the first-aid kit of a police car, but she probably needs to dip her entire face into salt water to make sure she gets all of the dust out of her eyes. She can't see very well at the moment as much because she can't use her contact lenses as from the concrete dust. Please reassure Hope that Angela has not a scratch on her, although I think her camera may be irreparably damaged."

"The police are there with you now, right? Did they find the shooter? How do you think he found you in the cemetery? Your visit there was a spur of the moment decision, so who followed you from the hotel there?"

"You sound like a cop," Jill said with a smile in her voice. Now that she knew for sure that they were not going to die, she could smile about the situation. "Detective Ireland and I are trying to answer those questions. I'm hoping we'll be able to leave here in about thirty minutes."

"Text me when you're leaving the cemetery and continue to take care of yourself and your friends. Love you, babe."

Jill saw the detective approaching and said, "Back at you," and ended the call.

Detective Ireland looked at Angela, checking out her camera and asked her, "Does it still work, or is it damaged?"

"Yes, to both questions. The camera itself works, but my telephoto lens is toast. I don't think the bullet damaged it, but the camera landed face down on the lens on this concrete, and so there's a crack in it. I think the wind of the bullet racing by knocked the camera over. When I get home, I'll have my camera specialist see if the lens can be repaired. I travel with extra lenses, so I have another one back at the hotel I can use on this camera."

The detective gave her a look to say that it was better the lens than your head, and Angela likewise gave him a nod back, confirming the thoughts he communicated in his facial expression.

"I need the three of you to help direct the crime scene staff on where the bullets might possibly be. Then I'll need to interview each of you for a statement, and you'll be free to go. Once the patrol car returns from dropping off your friends, I'll have it drive you back to the hotel. I will make a call to the hotel security, notifying them that threats have been made against some of their guests."

The three friends turned out to be pretty good witnesses to the shooting. They were able to locate the other bullets in the cemetery in record time despite the dim light of dusk. Detective Ireland interviewed them, and they left the cemetery soon after that. The crime scene team continued to search the grounds for the shell casings. Fortunately, they were made from copper and easily detected by metal detectors.

CHAPTER 10

The living room of the hotel suite was filled with all of their friends when Jill, Marie, and Angela returned from the cemetery. Hope took Angela in her arms after first looking at her to make sure nothing was out of place.

"Mom, I'm fine. Really. Jill's cases can be dangerous, but we always come out of them mostly without a scratch. Speaking of scratches, Jo, how are your eyes?"

Jo was looking at them through glasses with reddened eyes and said, "My eyesight is back, and now my eyes are mostly just tired. I think that they'll be fine in the morning."

Jill was standing inside of Nathan's arms and said, "That's good, and if your eyes weren't better by the time we returned, I was going to recommend that you head to a hospital, and have an ophthalmologist look at them."

"I don't have health insurance for Canada, so I'd rather not touch the Canadian health care system, and since I can see, I don't need to."

"So, what happened?" Henrik asked, looking Marie up and down for damage to her person. "I just entered the suite about five minutes ahead of you. I heard there were shots fired in the ceme-tery. What's going on?"

"Let me grab a glass of wine and I'll tell you what happened," Jill said, sitting down while Nathan furnished her with her liba-tion of choice.

Taking a sip and sighing, she said, "The cemetery is huge, and the creepy weather as Jo called it, likely saved our lives. We visited both graves, but each gravesite marker had to be cleaned as there was grass overgrowing it, so we spent a little more time at each location than we expected. The wind is really blowing out there with estimated wind gusts of forty miles an hour. That meant there were frequent moments of blowing leaves, and a few big tree branches were cracking as the wind was breaking them."

"Oh my," said Hope.

"Yes, imagine those sights and sounds in a huge cemetery as the light was slowly dimming at the end of the day. Perfect set-up for a horror movie," Jill said with a smile. "Before we were shot at, Jo declared that the cemetery was creepy. So we finished clearing the grass around my grandmother's grave when at first we thought it was a branch cracking, but then I told everyone to duck because I knew what that sound meant, and it wasn't a tree branch breaking. I called the detective from my cell phone as we took cover behind some tall memorial stones. We began weaving toward the exit taking cover behind large memorials as we went. Jo's luck ran out as the third and final shot rang out. It hit the concrete just above her head, which showered particles into her eyes, and she was blinded. Fortunately, the patrol car arrived about then. A police siren makes an incredible amount of noise inside a cemetery, and so our shooter had plenty of time to take off and did. The police used an infrared camera to search for the gunman, but no one else was alive in the cemetery. We gave statements and helped the crime scene team to round up the bullets and shell casings, and then we were dropped off here with a warning about hotel security."

Henrik's attention perked up with the comments about hotel security, and he said, "So the police think that your assassin followed you there from this hotel, correct?"

"I asked myself who could've followed me to the cemetery? Given the last-minute nature of our decision to go there, either the shooter was watching the hotel for us to leave, or they paid off the doorman to find out where we hailed the taxi to. It's the only conclusion that makes sense. Shooting at five strangers in a cemetery isn't the typical behavior of a serial killer, and that causes me to conclude that we were targeted."

"So how did they know that you were even involved with this case?" asked Hope.

"We gave some thought to that key question. The only answer we could come up with was someone watched us the day of the murder inside the church or watched Marie and I today explore the church. I'm not sure why we would be targeted over the detectives except that we're unarmed. But even if we were shot and killed, the investigation would still continue, so I'm not sure I understand the reasoning here, but that's the conclusion we came to."

"Do you know what kind of gun was used to shoot at you?" asked Henrik. He had an extensive collection of guns and was rather an expert at makes, models, and calibers.

"We heard on our way back to the hotel, that the Canadian gun experts identified it as a 54 mm Mosin rifle."

Henrik immediately understood why that was such bad news and said, "That's a Russian-made rifle used by snipers. I don't think they were a very good sniper if they missed hitting you three times."

"Actually, it was probably an outstanding shooter aiming at us, and it was the forty mile-per-hour wind gusts that saved us from being more injured then Jo is at the moment."

"What's a Mosin rifle?" Nathan asked, picking up on Henrik's concern.

Jill didn't know much about guns, and so she looked over at Henrik as the expert in the room.

"The Mosin is a Russian-made sniper rifle that is no longer manufactured. It's routinely still used by special forces troops in Russia and countries that Russia has supplied with arms. It's considered to be a good hunting rifle. A 54 mm bullet is considered big enough to bring down any game in North America." The unspoken comment in the suite was that it was also big enough to kill the five of them.

"So what you're saying is that while investigating the death of a Russian pianist, my adopted daughters and the real one are being chased by a Russian sniper. Is my assessment correct?" asked Hope.

"I would say that you stated that correctly," Jill agreed.

"Well, if they brought their big guns to the party, we have to bring ours."

"But... We don't have any guns with us in Canada. In fact, some of us don't even own guns," Marie said.

"I think your brains are bigger guns than this Mosin rifle. Nathan and I will finish up with the dinner preparations and set the table. All of you just use your heads to solve this murder," Hope said, fluttering her hand at the room as she stood up to head to the kitchen. She'd been watching Nathan cook earlier and knew they could easily have the meal on the table in thirty minutes. "Think hard and fast because we are serving dinner in thirty minutes."

They all grinned up at her, and Nathan stood to join her in the kitchen.

Angela looked around the group and grinned, "Well, I guess we have our marching orders. We have thirty minutes to solve this attempted murder. Let's put our collective brains together."

They began tossing ideas out on how they could identify the shooter and the motive behind his or her actions.

"Angela, let's pull up your photographs of the church at the time of the murder and make sure we run them through the facial recognition software. Jo and Marie, I don't think you can do much until we get the real name of our suspect Voldemar Tamm. Henrik, you have your giant computer trying to identify who Mr. Tamm is, do you think you have any early information? Or does your company only get a report at the end of all those computations? What else should we be doing?"

"This chain of hotels that we're staying in signed a contract with my company to handle their security. I think I can have my staff tap into the videos of the outside door to see who followed you from this hotel to the cemetery," Henrik suggested.

"That's an awesome idea. While you work on getting that video footage for us, let's have a conversation about what we do if Voldemar Tamm or anyone else is found lurking outside of this hotel's front door. The Toronto Police are going to talk to hotel security, but I'm worried about everyone's safety," Jill said.

"I'll alert my Stuttgart headquarters and have them keep an eye on the video surveillance around this hotel and this floor. They're probably already doing that as part of a protection protocol anytime I travel, but we have an actual threat that we need to guard against."

"Okay, your thirty minutes are up. Why don't we eat dinner now?" Hope suggested. "Everyone's brains work better with a good meal."

Jill stood up and said, "That's a brilliant idea. I'm starving, and my brain will be addled if I drink any more wine on an empty stomach. Do you need any help in the kitchen?"

She got three simultaneous 'nos' in response to her question. She was a brilliant chemist and vintner, but no one wanted her in the kitchen. She just smiled and took a seat at the suite's dining table while everyone joined her, except Nathan and Hope who began placing food on the table.

Angela took a moment to say an extended Grace, and they all dug into the delicious meal.

Both Jill and Henrik received texts and email during the meal, but Jill wanted a peaceful dinner and so firmly kept the conversation focused on Niagara Falls and their upcoming trip to the province of Québec. She wasn't surprised to find that Henrik spoke French. Most Europeans could speak several languages, and he was no exception. He also had a smattering of Mandarin and Japanese. Jill had made several attempts to learn a second language by taking French in high school and college. Later, while being around Spanish speakers in California, she'd attempted to use an app to learn that language. In the end, she wasn't fluent in any language other than English. Angela had more of a knack of picking up foreign words with the right enunciation.

With the excellent dinner finished, they resumed their positions on the sofas and chairs in the living room of the suite. Jill and Henrik took a moment to share their emails with the team.

"My people are quicker than I expected them to be. We have confirmation that Voldemar Tamm has been identified by the hotel's cameras. We've identified a second person that he spoke to who isn't on the hotel staff. That second person got in his own car and followed your taxi for at least one-hundred yards after he left the hotel, and then it went out of the range of the camera. We're working on identifying the individual. There's a third individual that Tamm has spoken to, but we've been unable to get a full picture of that individual. My people also verified that they're watching the cameras on this floor and elsewhere in the hotel. So we have additional protection to the on-site hotel security."

"Constable Thompson dropped off a flash drive with footage from around the church during today's visit. It's at the lobby desk. Should we go fetch it or have someone bring it up?" Jill asked, thinking about their vulnerabilities inside the hotel.

"Let me go fetch it," Nathan said. "I don't think I'm well known to be connected to you, Jill, just yet. We met briefly in front of the church yesterday, but we haven't been seen together today. So I'm safe."

She nodded as he left the suite to run the errand.

"Why did Russia want your pianist dead?" Hope asked.

"That is the $64,000 question," Jill said.

She could see Henrik's puzzlement over her expression, and so explained, "There was a game show in the 1950s called the $64,000 question, now it's just an American expression to say that's the big question."

He nodded his recognition of her explanation, "Das Leben ist kein Ponyhof, which translates to life is not a pony farm meaning that we will have to work hard for the answer to Hope's question."

"No offense, ladies, but Russia rarely takes an ad out in a newspaper to tell us what they're up to with their spies or even their piano players," Jack said.

"That just means we have to spy on them. We've figured out difficult motives in the past, and we'll do so with this case," Angela said, holding out her fist.

Soon her three friends leaned in to bump her fist, with Marie adding, "All for one, one for all."

She looked at Henrik, smiled, and added, "Alexander Dumas, The Three Musketeers."

"Ah," he said with a grin enjoying the spirit of his friends, as Nathan re-entered the suite, flash drive in hand.

"So, how are you to spy on them?" Hope asked.

"My preferred method is to follow the money, but before I do that, I need all the possible aliases that the pianist, Mr. Tamm, and our other unknown guy use. I already researched our pianist and didn't find anything unusual. So get me some more names and some names of the people around our pianist, and I'll trace the money inside Russia hopefully. There has to be payments for his performances. At the same time, I agree with you, Jill, that this was a crime of passion. So who did our pianist insult, or disappoint, or somehow raise the emotion in someone else?"

"Okay, Jo, I'm going to have my people do a specific search on Mr. Tamm to see what names he's entered countries under. Marie and Jo, perhaps the two of you could do a business search and find any businesses related to our pianist or our suspect. Does our pianist have an agent?" Henrik asked. "I assume that they have such a role in Russia, and perhaps that agent handled any extraordinary payments to the pianist."

"I'm going to borrow your laptop, Jill, and run every picture I've taken from about an hour before Mr. Chernov's murder to now. Who knows, maybe someone followed us today to Niagara Falls?" Angela said. "Jack, can you help edit each picture, so I have the best face possible for the software search?"

"Hope and I are going to put our heads together and come up with a delicious dessert for all of you," Nathan said. "Until you all figure this case out, I don't think we should be ordering from room service."

After the round of applause for the dessert, Jill said, "You are so brilliant, sweetie. I'm going to call Detective Ireland to see what they learned about Mr. Chernov from searching wherever he stayed for the past couple of nights. Surely, there have to be some clues there."

Heads down, they all chose their separate path to find the killer. Nathan and Hope could be heard discussing dessert in the kitchen, then pans and utensils were rattling.

Jill had gone to her bedroom to talk to the detective while Henrik likewise stepped outside on the hotel balcony so that their phone conversations wouldn't distract everyone else working on their own assignments.

"Detective, it occurred to me that I don't have some information from you on this case. Can you tell me what you found when you searched Mr. Chernov's hotel room? Did you find any source of arsenic there? Did your officers search the hotel room or interview any people at the previous lodgings that he stayed at?"

She heard a sigh on the other end of the line, "Just a moment. I have to switch my notes from tonight's shooting to the previous case."

Poor man, he had a long day that apparently wasn't over yet. He must be at work in the detective's division. She heard keyboard clacking, so he must've set his phone down close by to answer Jill's questions.

"Our crime scene technicians discovered arsenic in an allergy medication. It was a prescription antihistamine that our victim would've sprayed into his nose. It would've made his allergies worse, and perhaps he took even more of it because of that side effect, and there's a comment that it would've been absorbed faster through the nasal membrane. He actually contacted his doctor back in Russia with the complaint that he felt like he always had a cold. We found an email message on his phone. My team estimates that he would have died by his Montréal concert given the concentration of arsenic in the bottle."

"Did your crime scene staff say how difficult it is to put arsenic in a liquid?" Jill thought she knew the answer to her own question, but she was curious as to whether the crime scene staff commented on that. Arsenic was present in water systems across the world, so putting it in a liquid was a great idea by whoever was poisoning the victim.

She could hear him clicking a mouse searching for the answer, and a moment later, he said, "Oh, this is ingenious. Apparently, the bottle that the antihistamine came in was lined with arsenic metal. The liquid antihistamine was the real deal inside the bottle. Again our killer is smart and has access to the purchase of arsenic lined bottles. That's not something your average citizen anywhere in the world can go out and purchase. We think that the killer had access to Mr. Chernov's possessions at some point, and he substituted one bottle for the arsenic bottle."

"Yes, that certainly is a brilliant way to poison someone, and since our suspect is Russian and we were shot at earlier by a Russian-made gun, I think this bottle was also manufactured in Russia. We likely have no hope of tracing it. What else did your team find?"

"We fingerprinted the bottle, his toothbrush and razor, and a hairbrush. As you can imagine, a hotel room is filled with fingerprints, and so we only dusted those items that we thought might contain only his fingerprints or someone close to them like the mysterious wife we haven't yet traced."

"And the results of that fingerprinting? I would have thought you would have results by now."

"We found our victim's on these items, but we haven't identified the other fingerprints."

"That's surprising as fingerprints are taken as part of the passport process to enter the US. I don't know what Canada's requirements are, but I assume they're close to the U.S."

"I can't compare the two countries as I don't know all of our rules and regulations, but we also require fingerprints to get a travel visa to Canada. So either the person that touched these items is a Canadian who has managed to never give their fingerprints to the government, or we simply haven't found the right database to match them to, or there's an error in our fingerprint system that we haven't discovered yet."

"Can you send me the fingerprints that your crew hasn't matched yet? Maybe we can do something with them," Jill requested.

"Your Mr. Klein is a man of many talents if he can get results on these prints."

"I'm lucky to have him as a friend and as a colleague. His technology has made me a more effective private investigator. It doesn't solve the crime for me, but it usually aids me and having a more accurate list of players and suspects in any case. He jokes that he wants to hire me as a marketing VP, but I always tell him that his system sells itself as law enforcement gets results out of it. Was there any other finding from the hotel room of our victim?"

"No. Nikita was a bit of a slob, and there was sheet music everywhere, but no piano or keyboard to practice on."

"My limited knowledge of piano players suggests that the great ones don't practice on anything but a concert piano. The pressure that they place on the keys is so important, and this can be different than what happens with a keyboard."

They wrapped up the conversation, and Jill noted the arrival of an email with the fingerprints that she'd asked for.

Angela was sorting through the photographs on her camera. As a professional photographer, she always had far more pictures than the average person, and her activity over the last couple of days was no different. She'd taken over two-hundred photographs over the previous two days. Usually, she edited them once she arrived home from a vacation. She might shoot the same picture five to seven times, trying to get the perfect composition, so it appeared that she had lots of duplicates. However, her artist's eyes could detect the difference in the pictures.

As people were important in these photographs, she had to pick the best picture with a clear face, rather than the overall composition. She and Jack worked through the images, slowly reducing their numbers to about fifty faces. She had no idea how long it would take to match people to their name as she had never used Henrik's software before. She was pleasantly surprised that each picture was taking less than a minute to come up with iden-tification.

"The system's working fast. I think that must be because I picked the pictures with the clearest faces to run through Henrik's program. The software had an easier time deciding whether my faces in the pictures match to someone else in the world."

"We did do a good job of isolating these faces in the broader context of the picture, and that made it easier for the computer to do its work," Jack said.

"I'll save this whole list for Jill to go over, but I'll take half, and you take half. Let's decide if there's anything unusual in the back-ground of these individuals. If there is, Marie and Jo can take a gander at their backgrounds."

Many of the faces were easy to eliminate as were citizens of

Toronto or Niagara Falls and had jobs in those cities. Angela had the feeling that their suspect was from another country - likely Russia. In the end, she whittled down the list to four people. One of them had a Russian last name while the other three were born in Russia. She passed the names over to Jo and Marie, and they went to work digging into the financial and social backgrounds of the three Russians.

Jill returned to the living room of the suite armed with her new information and ready to check on what her friends to come up with. Angela returned her laptop to her, and Jill looked for the option of searching for a fingerprint rather than facial recognition. She was sure that Henrik had built something that useful into the software; she just had never tried to use it in the past.

"So, what did you find?" Jill asked.

"We looked at over fifty faces but focused our attention on four of them. There was a male and a female unrelated, both here on tours with tourist visas from Russia. The other two are also Russian citizens, but the guy is the conductor for the Toronto Philharmonic Orchestra, and the woman is his spouse. I think we can probably eliminate them as I find it hard to think of them having a motive to kill Mr. Chernov."

"It does seem unlikely that someone working as the conductor for that group would have it in them to do this complicated murder scenario that we have. Let's not eliminate the couple, but we will move them to the bottom of our suspect list. So it's on to Marie and Jo to figure out these two people with the tourist visas."

Nathan and Hope had served a warm brownie with vanilla ice cream. It was divine, and the sugar boost gave her renewed energy to chase down her fingerprints. Just as she started searching for instructions on how to match fingerprints, Henrik reentered the room from the balcony, and so she called him over for a quick lesson. In no time at all, she saw the spinning symbol, which was a sign that the computer was thinking. She relaxed by the coffee table so she could devote her full attention to the dessert.

"My staff are brilliant. They found six aliases for Mr. Tamm." Henrik said, and watched every head in the room turn toward him. He copied the names down on several pieces of paper and distributed them to Jo and Marie. "They also give me a partial match on the second person outside of this hotel."

"What's a partial match?" Jo asked, imagining the computer matching nose to nose but being unhappy with the lips of a face.

"A partial match is a match that's between 70% and 80% confidence. Most pictures are matched at over 95%. In this scenario, it's worth looking at. Also, the hotel is being observed, but the watchers haven't got within range of the cameras, but my staff is on it."

"If you can't identify the men watching, how do you know they are watching us?" Hope asked.

"Good question, Mom," Marie said waiting for someone to answer.

"The cameras caught our Mr. Tamm chatting with the other car at some point," Henrik replied.

Jill's laptop beeped, signifying that the fingerprint search was completed.

"What are the alias names for our Mr. Tamm?" Jill asked Henrik.

She reviewed the list against the fingerprints on the antihistamine bottle and said, "One of his aliases is on the bottle. Is your software something that can be used in court as evidence, or can the crime lab duplicate it if we point them that way?"

"Yes, of course. My system uses nothing more than powerful computing, but it's based on whatever is already out in the world. My software is updated from sources around the world twice a day, so as new fingerprints or pictures are entered into reliable databases, my software is likewise updated."

Henrik's voice indicated he was a little miffed with Jill's questions on accuracy and reliability, so she sought to soften its impact.

"Just gathering positive descriptive words from you for when I assume my role as your marketing VP," she said with a smile, and she was pleased to see his hackles relax. "I guess I better call the detective again."

She finished the final bites of her dessert and picked up her cell phone to call the detective.

"Yes?" the detective said when he answered his phone. He piled lots of meaning into that single word. His voice said he wasn't happy to hear from her, but he also had a tone that said he knew the news was coming his way, and the question was, would it be good news or bad?

CHAPTER 11

"Through the magic of computers, we've been able to locate multiple aliases for our Mr. Tamm, and the fingerprints for one of those aliases was on the antihistamine bottle."

"Wow. That's quite a piece of evidence. I think I'd better come over and meet you. I presume you're at the same location as last night?"

"Yes."

"Be there in thirty."

Jill looked at the clock and decided it was likely going to be a late-night for all of them. The detective would arrive roughly about 9pm. "The detective is going to arrive in about thirty minutes. Do we have any dessert we can share with him? The poor guy probably just got home from the scene at the cemetery, and hasn't had time to eat yet."

"We do have extras, so if he brings anyone with him, we can feed them too," Nathan said. Hope nodded at his reply while she continued crocheting a sweater.

Jill leaned over Marie and Jo to see how it was going with the identification of people. Jo hadn't found anything on Mr. Tamm, and now she understood why – it was a fake name that he used for purposes other than paying bills. With Henrik's list in hand, Jo had begun searching the alias names for information. "So this name that is attached to the fingerprints appears to be his real name, Andrei Danilov, right?"

"Yes, what did you find on him?" Jill asked.

"I just started searching, but it's going to be slow. Everything has to be translated into English. They use a different accounting system in Russia, but that's mostly corporate finance, not the reports of how Russian citizens do their banking. There's poor transparency, so I doubt I'm going to find anything on anyone. I would be better served helping Marie do her thing."

"I don't disagree with you, Jo. By the way, I'm going to keep calling him Mr. Tamm as that is easier for me to pronounce than his real name. Marie, have you found anything new with any of Mr. Tamm's names?" Jill asked.

"Jeez, I've only had the names for five minutes. You're expecting miracles here."

"Well, was there a miracle? Do you have a breakthrough?"

"Not yet. Mostly because I started to work on the first one on Henrik's list, which wasn't the alias that might be his real name with the fingerprints. There's a Facebook profile on the first name that appears to have been active for about five years but went dormant about two years ago. There's a Russian Facebook company called VK, which is short for Vkontakte, and there was a profile there with basically the same information. Now I'll move on to Andrei Danilov."

Jo and Angela assisted Marie by searching for some of the other aliases. Henrik excused himself for the night to get work done but leaned down to kiss Marie before he left the suite for their own. Nathan and Hope had their heads together compiling menus for the next day, though they were supposed to leave late for Montréal.

Almost to the minute, they heard a knock on the suite door.

Nathan opened the door to Ireland, Kim, and Hassan. Jill was surprised to see Ireland's colleagues, but then again, he'd had a long day dealing with her, the autopsy, and the cemetery shooting.

Jill seated them at the dining table while Hope brought them the dessert. Who could turn down such a splendid smelling dessert from an older woman?

"So Henrik's company did some identification work in Stuttgart where they have big powerful computers. They searched the world for Mr. Tamm's face and found it under a variety of passports and other names. One of those passports, under the name Andrei Danilov, had fingerprints attached to his passport, and those fingerprints were matched by Henrik's software program to the fingerprints you provided me, Detective, on the anti-histamine bottle. Angela also processed her pictures over the last few days and found five Russians in her photographs. Maybe it's a coincidence and maybe not," Jill said, then she had a small smile at the rate that all of the desserts disappeared.

The three detectives took a look at the fingerprint matches and the alias pictures.

"Can you send this to us?" asked Hassan.

"Of course. Do you also want the Russian names we encountered at the church and beyond?"

"I would hate to focus on one group of people simply because of their country of origin. In Toronto, we have over 100,000 Russians living in our city. So the law of averages would say that you would cross this ethnicity in your daily movement across the city," said Detective-Sargent Hassan.

Jill was disappointed with his answer. She had a gut feeling that Russia was behind this murder. They murdered people all over the world who disagreed with their president. There was the man in England who, along with his daughter, was exposed to a nerve agent. A journalist who wrote of problems with the current Russian administration died in Berlin. Creating a bottle lined with arsenic was more than your average killer was capable of, and it said Russia all over it. Just when she thought she was gaining respect from the Canadian law enforcement officials, they discounted her theories. Usually, it was two steps forward and one step back. In this case, she felt like it was two steps forward and four steps back.

"Okay then, I guess we're done. We leave for Montréal tomorrow evening, and so I wish you, detectives, good luck in solving this murder," Jill said, standing up to lead them to the suite's door.

The three officers looked a little nonplussed at Jill's dismissal of them, but then they stood up thanking Hope for the dessert, and the room cleared out in under three minutes.

"Yowza, I feel a Northern Territory arctic blast blowing through this hotel suite. Jill, you practically physically tossed them out of the suite, and I can see that you're boiling mad about something," Nathan said. "It must have been that they didn't take you seriously. That's what usually sets you off."

Nathan's comment further enraged her as his words made it sound like she was being petty, and she knew she wasn't.

"I know the Russians are behind this entire situation. They've got the science, resources, and manpower to pull off Mr. Chernov's death and the shooting at the cemetery."

"I don't disagree with you, Babe, but I understand his position. Cops are heavily criticized if they target a specific ethnicity for crimes. It would not look good if he stood up at a press conference and said he knows in his heart that a Russian did it, but can't explain his thinking beyond that point. The public thinks his gut feeling is just another word for bias or prejudice," Nathan said.

"You have a lot of random facts that you can see add up to the big picture, but few have your insight, training, or experience. He'll come around to your thinking," Jo said. "Even if you do nothing more on this case, most of the detective work so far has been done by you."

"I think he'll run with your information, Jill. Like Nathan said, he can't admit to targeting people of a certain country, but that won't stop them in evaluating the situation," Marie said.

"But he didn't ask the names of the people in Angela's pictures. So there's no way he can follow up on that clue," Jill said. "I'm going to go to bed as there's nothing more to be done tonight. We'll be sightseeing in Toronto tomorrow and then heading for Montréal in the evening. Thanks, everyone, for your help."

There was silence in the room as everyone understood why Jill was so mad. The detectives left the suite without the names of additional suspects, and she considered that a critical piece of evidence.

"So, what are you guys going to do now?" Hope asked, sitting down in the spot that Jill vacated.

"Mom, there's nothing we can do now. Jill's our team leader, and she just declared that the case was done for us."

"Darn, I was just getting somewhere," Marie said. "I kept researching while everybody else was talking, and I found our pianist's agent. I was hoping to pass that on to Jo to see if she could do anything with the information."

"I'm not ready to go to sleep. I'll look the agent up, and maybe there's a company behind the agent that will tell us something."

"You know what else she didn't tell the detectives?" Nathan said. "She forgot to tell them that this hotel is being watched by men. I don't think you're all safe until you solve this case. So I think you all need to continue working tonight until you find who's behind this whole thing. Otherwise, you all are going to have to look over your shoulders tomorrow while you're sightseeing. The shooter was lucky tonight because the cemetery was empty, but tomorrow there will be people everywhere, and that should provide you with some security. I'm going to go talk to Jill and suggest that despite the lack of respect she feels from the detectives, that she needs to lead this group to ensure everyone's safety because even though the cops have given up on you, the bad guys haven't."

Angela, Jo, and Marie couldn't remember another time when Nathan gave them the pep speech to keep an investigation going. His work on their cases was never analytical. Instead, he kept an eye out for their safety, and he was right, they weren't safe. The good guys weren't paying attention, and the bad guys were ready to attack them.

Marie leaned forward with her fist and repeated her earlier words, "All for one and one for all." After the fist bump, they went to work.

A few minutes later, Jill appeared in a jogging suit hastily put on over her nightshirt. "Sorry guys, I was so angered by the detectives, I forgot about our watchers. Now, we're working on the case for ourselves, not for Mr. Chernov, or the police, or for the American Embassy. This is about us being safe in Canada, and having no more shootouts in cemeteries."

Everyone nodded and went back to searching for information on their computers. There was silence in the room, and then broken by a sudden flurry, there would be a flurry of clacking on a keyboard. Hope was working on her sweater in silence, while Nathan was using a mouse for some kind of graphic design for a wine label.

Jo asked, "Jill, can you do a diagram on the dry erase board of all the people we've sourced as suspects or relatives of the victim? I think I might've found an unusual payment to Mr. Chernov's parents, but I can't remember their names, and it occurs to me that it would help to have all these Russian names on one page."

"That's a good idea. I'll admit I have a hard time keeping the names straight. I'm going to write it on the poster board, so we can tape it to the wall here for reference. I don't think I know the names of Nikita's parents. Perhaps Marie came across that in her research."

Marie looked up with the mention of her name. She'd been chasing her own information and wrote down where she was on the search, so she could find it again.

"Let me see, his parents' names are Pavel Mikhailovich Chernov and Tatiana Kimova Borodina. Apparently, in this family, the wife didn't take the husband's name. She must have established her reputation under her own name as a musician."

"Wow, those are long names. Okay, there is a large payment from the agent's company to the parents."

"What is large in this case?" Jill asked.

"Ten million Russian rubles which translates to a little over $150,000 in US dollars. There also appears to be two apartment payments by the agent for the Chernovs."

"Maybe those were his earnings as a pianist?" Angela suggested.

"I don't think so as I don't see any other payments over the past decade," Jo said. "And why the payment for apartments? Maybe that's a common Russian way of making payment."

"Do we have a way of checking to see if the paperwork was ever filed for U.S. citizenship?" Jill asked Marie. "I know you said that you found no record of him being an American citizen, but was there an application going forth? Was it just this concert announcement that said he was an American. Is there any way we can find out if programs from his previous performances listed his country of origin?"

"What does US citizenship have to do with anything?" asked Hope.

"I don't know, but why would you lie about that if you're a concert pianist? Being from the land of Tchaikovsky is probably a good thing in the piano world. So was he trying to move out of Russia permanently, or was that a typo in the recital announcement? Jo, can you tell where the money came from that was deposited into the agent's account so it could then be paid to the Chernovs?"

Jill and Angela were staring at the piece of paper with all the Russian names on it, thinking. Marie and Jo were typing and reading, then typing faster and pausing to read.

"It's going to take me a while to follow the money trail on this payment to the Chernovs. There's one false trail after another. This is kind of fun, I love chasing people who try to hide money."

"I don't have access to the State Department to understand if he filed the paperwork to become a citizen, but I went back and looked at a bunch of his Facebook and VK postings, and there's no mention whatsoever about changing citizenship. Then again, if you're living in mother Russia, that might be a dangerous thing to say. I also looked at the previous concerts he gave on this tour, and I don't see any mention of him being an American. I think we have to consider that aspect of this case as a typo on the part of the church."

"Okay," Jill agreed that there wasn't anything more they could do with that piece of information.

"How about the wife? Is there anything more we can do with that piece of information?"

"Is there a picture of her? Maybe you could run her through your software to see where she pops up." Angela suggested.

"I should have thought of that before now. That's a brilliant idea, Angela. Marie, can you find that post and send it to me? If her picture doesn't turn up anywhere, and it might not if she hasn't left Russia, then we likely know that she's not a suspect," Jill said.

"Jack, maybe you'd better edit this photo for me. I noticed the search went much faster with Angela's photos when you did that."

Jack taught graphic arts at a college in Wisconsin and was the best editor for film or video that Jill had ever come across. A few minutes later, he had created a far better picture then what she started with.

She scanned the picture into her software and said to Jack, "If the paparazzi ever discovered how good you are at photo editing, they would be on you in a flash to enhance their celebrity pictures."

"No, thanks. I've no desire to work for such disreputable

people. Instead, I teach the next generation to work for them. However, I do try to steer my students towards advertising firms rather than the paparazzi," Jack said with a grin.

Hope looked up from her crocheting and smiled at him benignly. Jill could almost feel the words, 'good boy'.

"This is interesting," Jill said and walked over to the dining room's dry erase boards. "She entered the United States at the same time our victim did. They must've flown here together."

"Does she appear between the border of the United States and Canada? Or did she drop out of sight after entering the United States?" Angela asked.

"It looks like her one and only appearance in front of any security camera was to leave Russia and fly nonstop to New York City. Did Mr. Chernov start his performances in New York City? I don't remember all of his performance dates and cities."

"Maybe we should look at the crime report in New York City to see if any Russian woman has been murdered there in the past month or two," Maria suggested.

"You've been working for Jill too long if your first thought is that she's dead," Jo said.

"I have been working for Jill too long as it's my gut feeling that she's also dead, which points to her being dead in NYC," Marie said.

"Okay, I'll look for that information. Jill, why don't you look at the crime reports of the other cities he played in. I see Detroit, Chicago, and Newark, which is close to NYC," Angela said. An idea occurred to her, and she did a quick keyboard search. "Those are all cities with large Russian populations. All that's missing from his tour list is Los Angeles, Vancouver, and Calgary, and he would've hit all the major North American cities with the most Russians. Perhaps his agent was still trying to line up those cities."

"Do we know how old Anna Chernov is?" Angela asked. "I presume I'm looking for some anonymous dead female between the ages of eighteen and twenty-five, or something like that."

"You're correct. According to my software, her passport says that Anna is twenty-four."

CHAPTER 12

After a search of cities, they found no reports of unidentified females that fit Mrs. Chernov's description, and there was no record of her crossing the border into Canada.

"I wonder if she melted into one of the Russian communities in Newark, Detroit, or Chicago? That might be what I would do if I wanted to escape Russia," Angela suggested.

"Or visit the State Department," offered Hope.

"Or turn yourself into a police department," said Jack.

"Perhaps she hired an attorney to represent her with Immigration and Naturalization. Maybe she's in the protective custody of the Marshal Service. My imagination can formulate all kinds of scenarios for her. Where is she?"

"Does she know her husband was murdered?" Jack added.

"Let's look at the newspapers to see if they carried the story," Jill said.

A moment later, they saw that it was carried in pretty much every newspaper in North America. It was such a sensational way to kill someone, they could understand the interest in this story. Then they looked at some Russian language newspapers and saw the story as well. She would've had to have been extremely isolated to not know her husband was dead.

"So how do you find out if she's in protective custody?" asked Hope. Angela's mother was becoming the out-loud voice for all the thinking that was going on in the room.

Jill's team thought about previous cases and couldn't think of when they needed help with the Marshal's Service except when Jill had been in protective custody in one of their initial investigations.

"Maybe I could contact the Marshals who protected me in one of our first cases?"

"Was that the Marshals, or did the FBI protect you? I don't recall meeting any Marshals," Nathan said.

Jill thought for a moment and then nodded, "I think you're right, Nathan. Maybe I haven't come in contact with the Marshals Service."

"Why not contact the FBI and use them to reach the Marshals Service?" Angela suggested. "Special Agent Ortiz has always been helpful."

"That's a good suggestion. Maybe she can direct Susan Garrett to assist us or just check out her own resources," Jill said, checking her watch to see what time it was on the west coast. "Darn, it's getting late. Perhaps she's not available to chat, I'll call it quits for the night and resume work in the morning."

She searched her contact list for Special Agent Ortiz's number and dialed.

"Hi Jill, are you having problems in Toronto?" the agent asked when she connected the call.

"How did you know? Are you FBI types psychic?"

"Agent Garrett and I chatted yesterday. I gave you great references, is she not cooperating?"

"No, nothing like that. She dropped off the case when it was determined that our victim wasn't an American citizen, and there appeared to be no threat to the U.S. It was a simple murder investigation."

"But you have an American question, now? Tell me about the case and where you are at this point. If I recall, it was a piano player that was killed with an ice arrow in a church during a performance. Actually, it played on all the American news stations as it was such a sensational killing. So what do you know that hasn't been broadcasted on the television?"

Jill relaxed into the conversation recounting what they had determined about the arsenic and her own near murder in the cemetery, and ending with her request for help with the wife's location.

"What an intriguing case. I understand why Agent Garrett stepped away as she's there to assist Canadians with the United States and Americans with Canada, not get involved in what appears to be a case limited to Canada in its entirety. So one idea that you have is the wife has sought protective custody in the United States, and the question is whether she's gone underground in a Russian community or if she's under U.S. Protection at the moment. I wonder if she had anything to offer about Russia? Our CIA would be interested in her, but if there's a plot afloat with the appearance of this Russian piano player, then it will be of interest to the FBI. Let me research this and get back to you. Is it okay if I call you back in the middle of the night if I have news? I realize you're on vacation, and there are others involved with any decisions you make."

Jill thought about getting a middle of the night call from the agent. It would wake Nathan up, but he'd be able to go back to sleep, unlike her. She would probably end up going out to the suite's living room and putting in some work on whatever information the agent could provide.

"Call me back day or night, the personal safety of eight people is on the line."

"That's an unusually large group. Did you hire more people?"

"No, we just included friends of friends this time. Not sure they'll want to vacation with us again."

"Okay, I'll get back to you."

The call ended, and there was no need to tell anyone in the room about her conversation as they had all heard her side of the phone call.

"So any idea of when she'll call back?" Marie asked. Like Jill, she was an early riser and ready to call it quits.

"It could be in ten minutes, and it might be in the middle of the night, or maybe tomorrow some time. I think us early birds should head to bed. I'll hear my cell phone from my sleep and wake up. If she wakes me up with information at one in the morning and may not be able to go back to sleep, or I may need to do something with the information, so this may be the only sleep I get in the night ahead. Anyone need anything before I go?"

There were head shakes indicating 'no'. Hope, Marie, Angela, and Jill headed for their respective bedrooms.

Jo looked at Jack, thinking about something, and then it came to her.

"Didn't you have a student you occasionally keep in touch with who works for the CIA?" Jo asked, trying to remember the story Jack had told her about this particular student.

"Yeah, I do. He graduated from my graphic arts program. He initially went to work in the video production area but has since made it up to the top echelon of the agency. He's the head of the Directorate of Digital Innovation. I've tried a few years ago to get him to return to Green Bay and lecture any semester of students, but he can never seem to get away from Langley, Virginia, which is the CIA's headquarters. I suppose you want me to contact him to see if his agency has a record of this Russian woman."

"Never hurts to approach a problem in two different ways. If Special Agent Ortiz can't help, maybe your former student can."

Jack looked through his contact list to see if he had former student Alex Whitehead's phone number with him. He noted that the number he had was a Green Bay area code, so the phone was probably disconnected. He decided to try anyway.

"Hello, Jack. Long time no hear from," Alex said when the call was connected.

"Yeah, it's been a while. So long, in fact, that I didn't think this call would go through as I doubted you still had a Green Bay number."

"No reason to change numbers. Besides, it makes it easy for old instructors to reach me. Sorry, but I still can't make it to one of your classes to lecture, the agency is keeping me very busy. So other than that, what can I do for you?"

"Actually, we need some help with the CIA."

"We?"

"It's a long story. What time zone are you in, perhaps I should call back at a reasonable hour."

"Are you kidding, Jack? You can't call me out of the blue and ask for my agency's help and also offer to call me back in the morning. What's up?"

"Are you in the eastern time zone at Langley?" Jack persisted.

"I can neither confirm nor deny that rumor," Alex said with humor in his voice.

Jack took a deep breath and plunged in with an explanation of what was happening. It took the better part of twenty minutes for Alex to get the full story. If he didn't know Jack so well, he wouldn't have believed the story, but while they talked, he was able to verify the identities of Jill, the Toronto police, and the murdered victim.

"What you're talking about is way outside my area of responsibility, but let me see if I can get the attention of someone inside the agency, and I'll get back to you. Should I call you on this cell phone?"

"Yes, and thanks, Alex."

"I owe you my current job; let me see if I can return the favor."

"You're always welcome to return to my class and lecture.

Maybe you'll find some new blood for your department," Jack added, always looking out for his students.

"That's a thought. Call you back when I have some information."

The call ended, and Jack stared dumbly at the phone for a few seconds.

"It's so bizarre being involved in one of Jill's cases. When you try to explain what you are all doing and what the problem is, you end up feeling stupid like the story you're telling couldn't possibly be true. But the story is so far-fetched that even I had trouble coming to terms with the shooting in the cemetery tonight."

Jo smiled and said, "That's life with Jill. I told you about the incident in the Sicilian Cave, where we were fighting off the Mafioso, right?"

Jack nodded.

"Well, that case reconfirmed that I belonged on this team, helping Jill. For a while, I was contemplating stepping off the team as I didn't like the dangerous stuff, but then I really thought about the good I do. It is so often beyond the dead person's immediate family, there's usually a bigger picture in the crime. The Mafioso has wrecked Sicily with its war on its own citizens through violence and bribery. We brought an end to that family, although there are still other families operating in Sicily. So besides getting justice for Randy Chen, we brought a little more sunshine to a region of Sicily, and I'm happy to do what I can to make that happen. It's sort of my charitable work. I mean, we do get paid, but we don't get paid enough for the risk to our lives."

Jack padded her on the knee and said, "I get it, and now I think it's time for us to go to bed and leave Nathan to his wine label projects."

Nathan had been bent over his laptop, moving his mouse in the creation of a marketing brochure design. When he was in the design zone, he was able to block out sounds around him, but he heard his name called out and looked up.

"Yes?"

"You're the last man standing, Nathan. Jack and I are heading to bed. Both Jill and Jack may get calls in the middle of the night from the CIA, so it may not be a restful night. You may want to try and catch some sleep now," Jo said, and she and Jack turned to leave the room.

"CIA? I thought Jill contacted the FBI. I guess I haven't been listening over the past hour or so."

"Jill contacted the FBI to contact the CIA for her, and Jack contacted a former student of his that happens to be high up in one of the administrative departments. Hopefully, one of those contacts will reach out to us soon."

"Oh, okay. I'll tell Jill if she wakes up when I enter our bedroom. Good night."

Nathan checked in with Henrik's staff to see if the hotel was still being watched, and it was. He supposed that Jack and Jo were correct; he ought to head to bed as it might not be a restful night.

CHAPTER 13

Andrei Danilov, who was going by the name of Voldemar Tamm while in Canada, was on the phone speaking in Russian as he sat on the side of his hotel bed. He yawned as it had been a long day followed by the long walk in the cemetery, and the hasty climb over the wall and into a residential yard. He was fortunate that he hadn't landed in a yard with dogs. He spotted the same cat that the woman had, and he watched it disappear, figuring that the yard it jumped into wouldn't contain dogs that would chase it or him. One of his men had replaced him at midnight to continue surveillance on the hotel where the woman doctor and her team were staying.

He received orders from Moscow to kill Mr. Chernov shortly after the pianist arrived in North America for recitals. Nikita, according to reports, was quite a brilliant pianist. He'd been all over the world performing and then had got too full of himself and had to scamper home to mother Russia to hide. Voldemar's agency moved in on him and his family, planning to make them useful. Apparently, the piano player was a little crazy, and that makeover took longer than expected. The plan had been for him to resume his brilliant career as a pianist aiming to play in the most exalted circles of North America.

First, he would have to overcome his reputation. Despite the brilliance of his fingers on the keyboard, cutting piano strings had sent him faster than a speeding bullet to the bottom of his career. When he hit bottom, it took some time to bring the giant ego down to view the basement of his career. When he finally understood that life with a piano as he had known it was over, Russia had its tentacles into him and his family, and now, they guided the next phase of his career. Their plan was to stage the comeback of his career. In a year or so, he would play in the White House, Rideau Hall in Ottawa, and the British Prime Minister's house in London. Russia had sophisticated listening devices they wanted to be planted in locations that only an entertainer like Mr. Chernov could reach. Russia also had a list of top political leader residences in North America, Europe, and China where they wanted the devices planted. They were tiny dust particles with ranges of a hundred meters. All the piano player had to do was stick his hand in a pocket of his coat or pants and come out with a fistful of these dust particles and fling them at walls, curtains, or carpet of the building hosting his performance. Once the music died down, Russia could listen to conversations occurring in those buildings. It was a brilliant plan, with years of research into the technology and training of the pianist to appropriately spread the particles. His parents had been paid generously for their son's participation in the scheme. Nikita had insisted on taking his wife with him on the first leg of this comeback tour. As directed, he spread dust particles in the churches that hosted his concerts along the way.

Each church Russia targeted, had one or more politicians among its congregation. As the concert locations became more prestigious, he would eventually find his way to places like the White House. Russia hoped that the American political targets would be indiscreet in church, and discuss secrets with their colleagues or spouses that attended with them. So far, they hadn't heard anything more than regular gossip. Then, at the last concert stop in Chicago before Nikita crossed the border into Canada, his wife Anna disappeared from sight, and they hadn't been able to locate her in the United States. His Russians keepers had placed trackers under the couple's skin so they could keep track of them while they moved about American and Canadian cities. Anna must've figured out how to damage the tracker because they had no trace of her. In reality, blocking the tracker was child's play. Sometimes, all you needed to do was cover the body part containing the tracker with foil to block a signal.

When they noticed her disappearance, they put plans in place to kill Nikita, knowing that neither he nor his wife were going to move forward with Russia's plan for them. If she defected to the United States, then this Russian operation would be exposed to much embarrassment. It had taken years to bring the operation to this point. The fruition of the Russian dream was fragile as they didn't trust the couple since the pianist was so volatile. Despite the threats made against his parents and his wife, Nikita always seemed just one second away from his ego making bad decisions for him.

The Federal Security Service or FSB for short, was on edge that they were about to be discovered, but there was only silence out of America. They wondered if Anna was still alive, and hoped she wasn't. The solution from Moscow came in the form of arsenic, but then they were getting impatient, and so ordered his murder accelerated. That fool Sergey had been practicing with ice arrows and convinced him to try it on a real target. He'd thrown Sergey under the bus to his superiors, saying he fired the arrow. That was fine, except they under-estimated the murder fascination in the western world. Chernov's death played in all the major newspapers in North America.

That was topped off with the colossal misfortune of having a forensic pathologist in the audience. Such bad luck, and especially this forensic pathologist. She did private investigative work internationally and had already taken down several of his countrymen. He tuned back into what was being said on the other side of the world into his phone.

"Do you have news of Anne Chernov's location?" asked Victor Milchenko, head of Counterintelligence for the FSB.

"No, we are searching for dead females in Chicago that are near to her description. We have informants in the Russian community there, and no one seems to be able to locate her."

"Could she be a guest of the Americans?"

"If so, why haven't we heard anything yet?"

"Maybe she is talking to them. We should have never enrolled Nikita into our informant program. He's been a disaster from the start. It took us longer than we expected to have him ready to return to North America. Then his wife defects, and your idiot shoots the man with an ice arrow, which was guaranteed to gain the attention of the world as an exotic death. I heard there was a doctor in this case that was a problem also. Who is he?"

"She's a doctor who was trained in autopsies. She privately consults to help detectives across the world, and she's already put a few of our countrymen in prison. From what I can tell, it was random bad luck. She was in the audience to enjoy the music and nothing more. Then she tried to comfort Nikita as he lay dying. The Canadian police are working with her. Her name is Jill Quint, if you want the FSB to research her."

"That's a terrible mistake. You and your men don't usually make those kinds of errors."

"You're right, we don't. I may be leaving Sergey behind in Canada as he's become such a liability. My plan is to get rid of the doctor and her team and dump their bodies into a lake around here since there are so many. I have surveillance on their hotel, and I managed to spread some of our special dust particles onto the jackets of her team members, so I've been listening in to their conversations."

"Have they seen you or your men?" Victor asked.

"Yes. They've been able to identify several of our passports and identities. They have a German man with them who has a software program that has analyzed our movements across borders around the world. They are a formidable opponent. The good news is that the Toronto police refused to target Russian citizens for this crime, and in doing so have severed the relationship with the doctor, and ignored some of our agents in the area."

"Andrei, this is much worse than I expected. Perhaps we should end all operations and return home, or at least have you leave North America, as your identity has been compromised. How many people are in this team surrounding the doctor?"

"There are a total of eight, including the German."

"Are all eight of them working on this investigation?"

"From what I've heard, most of them are working on the investigation. Some are tossing out random comments, while others are spending time on computers finding information."

"Andrei! This is unfortunate news. You and your men were assigned to watch the couple. We sent you an arsenic bottle to kill her husband, and instead, you accelerate his death in a way that was guaranteed to be news around the world. Now you're proposing to murder seven Americans and one German citizen and dump their bodies in a lake. Hopefully, you are planning to weigh them down so they would not be discovered. This operation has gone very bad very quickly. I don't think murdering seven Americans is the way to quiet things down. I'm going to discuss it with people here and will make the decision on your next steps. Do not do anything more than surveillance at this time. Do not kill anyone. Do not show your faces near any cameras. Go buy some masks as though you were afraid of germs to keep your faces covered at all times. I will get back to you, when I have an answer on what you should do with the doctor. Is that clear?"

"Yes, Comrade," Andrei responded. This was his twentieth year of working for the Russian Federal Security Bureau. He'd never seen an operation fall apart like this one had. Their volatile piano player had really screwed them up, and then his actions had thrown fuel on the fire they didn't want the West to see. He wondered if in six months, he would be working in a Siberian labor camp, or maybe he just might be dead.

The two Russians ended their call, and Andrei tried to quiet his racing mind knowing he needed some sleep to make better decisions then he and his team had made so far. He did one final check-in with his men on surveillance, advising them to take no action other than monitoring with the Americans. If they left for the airport in the middle of the night, his men were instructed not to intercept them, rather they should try to get on the same flight. He wanted to make sure his men understood that they had the cold and dreary duty of surveillance only until he heard back from Moscow.

CHAPTER 14

At four in the morning, Jack exited the bedroom he shared with Jo to answer his cell phone. She was not an early morning person, and he didn't want to disrupt her sleep.

He sat in the empty, dark living room of their luxurious hotel suite, and wondered what news his former student and now CIA employee had for him. He looked around for something to write on finding some hotel stationery and a pen.

"Have you been up all night researching my question? It's four in the morning here in Toronto, which means it's also four the morning in Virginia," Jack said to Alex Whitehead.

"I snagged a few hours of sleep in a crib, and we have four employees that are working extraordinary hours. It's like that when you work for the CIA."

"So what do you have for us?"

"We actually have a team on their way to you – they should be at your hotel by seven. But first, do you have a place you can go right now that's lead-lined?"

"What?" Jack asked, not sure he understood the request. "Can I put you on hold a second?"

Jack wasn't into these cases like Jo was, and he needed Jill's help immediately. He knocked on her door and approached her bed. He knew from Jo that she was a light sleeper, and so he motioned her out of the bedroom and into the suite. She grabbed a sweater to put on to ward off the chill of the suite overnight and followed him.

Once they were in the living room, he whispered into her ear, "I have a former student, Alex Whitehead, on the phone from the CIA, and he's asked me if we have a lead-lined place we can go to."

Jill knew immediately what the problem was. The CIA suspected there were bugs in the room. She thought for a moment and then grabbed a roll of foil from the kitchen and invited Jack to join her underneath the fume hood in the kitchen. She turned the stove hood on high, which made considerable noise in the suite, then wrapped a long piece of foil around her and Jack's head. She hoped the fan noise would drown out any bugs, and the foil would also insulate them. They looked stupid as heck, but a girl had to do what she needed to do, Jill thought with a grin.

"Hi Alex, it's Dr. Jill Quint. I lead this merry band of investigators. If you hear a noise, it's because Jack and I are standing close together with foil wrapped around us underneath a noisy hotel kitchen ventilation fan. We have no lead lining here, and so this was the best I could do. What's up?"

She could hear a man briefly laugh at the vision she gave him, and then said, "Hi Dr. Quint. I'm not sure you're in a secure spot, but thanks for trying. Take a picture and send it to me to make my day here at Langley. Do me a favor and answer my questions with yes or no."

"Ha!" Jill said convening that she knew she looked stupid, but still thought her efforts were better than the CIA man was giving her credit for.

"We have a team arriving at your hotel in three hours. We've arranged for two taxis to pick up your team and take you to a certain location that will be safe for conversations. I understand that you have a German security expert with you, and we would love to talk to him as well. Do you think you can wake your team up, ask them not to say anything about the case, and instead talk about visiting Rice Lake, which is to the north of you for a fishing expedition? You've all been dying to fish for perch and bass, and you've arranged for an excursion to do just that."

"Yes, thank you for calling. We're looking forward to our fishing excursion. I fished that lake as a child," Jill said as instructed, and they ended the call.

Jill unwrapped the foil and tossed it in the garbage. She gestured with her hands for Jack to stay under the hood while she went and got paper. He'd heard her side of the conversation and was puzzled about the fishing excursion. He never in his life heard her or her team talk about a love of fishing.

She wrote a note on the paper.

'The CIA has good reason to believe this hotel suite is bugged, so they need to take us elsewhere for a conversation. In the meantime, anything we say in the suite can be heard by whoever is listening. Show this note to Jo, and make sure she says nothing about the investigation and is ready to leave by seven.'

Jack looked at his watch and calculated that he would wake Jo up another hour. Jill would give Marie, Angela, and Nathan another hour and a half to sleep. She would text Henrik to make sure he was prepared to go, and she wasn't surprised when she got an immediate response that he and Marie would be ready at the designated time. It was the middle of the day in Germany, and he was likely getting some work done. It was probably the weirdest text he'd ever received from her given the instructions that he should wear clothing suitable to going out on a lake to fish. Knowing her history of getting in sticky situations she hoped; he assumed he was in the middle of one of them with her.

They turned the lights on in the suite, and then Jill said to Jack, "You couldn't sleep either?"

"No, I'm excited that we're renting a boat to go fishing. As you know, it was at the top of my list of things to do in Canada. Maybe after we fish in the lake, we can find a river and do some fly casting."

"Do you have waders and other clothing for fly fishing?"

"No, I didn't pack those items, but I do have my tackle box with my favorite lures to try on this lake."

Jill raised her eyebrows in worry. Jack might be taking the fishing conversation too far, for now he was going to have to show up at the hotel entrance with a tackle box.

"Do you want some coffee or tea?" Jill asked, approaching the kitchen.

"That would be great, let me help," and they approached the noisy fan again.

Jill whispered, "You're going to have to come to the entrance with a tackle box. Remember anything we say is being listened to, and the entrance is being watched."

Jack grinned, "Don't worry Jill, I've got you covered. Jo keeps her makeup and hair supplies in a tackle box. We'll be able to come to the hotel entrance carrying that box."

Jill grinned back at him, remembering the tackle box he was talking about. It was an excellent cover for this excursion.

They proceeded to chitchat first about fishing, which each of them had done enough times in their life to be able to talk about it, and then they moved on to his upcoming semester at the college and her new grape that she was growing.

They heard Marie come in from the suite door, an hour later.

"What are you guys doing up so early? Jack, I've never seen you awake at this hour before."

Jill held a finger to her mouth and motioned her to silence and beckoned Marie over to the kitchen fan, saying, "Come into the kitchen, and I'll get you some coffee. You can add what you need to it there."

Underneath the hood, she showed Marie the note she had

been going to use when she woke the others up in the bedroom. Marie looked at the note and nodded, looking a little worried. She usually remained optimistic about their survival during one of their cases. Still, news that the CIA would be running a covert operation with them in the middle of it upped the stakes of this case. Now it was time to slip into the role she would need to play for the next couple of hours.

"Jack, you're like a little boy excited at Christmas with this day of fishing in front of us. I've never been fishing, and I don't want to touch anything slimy or alive. What should I wear to be out on a boat? Also, I get seasick, should I take something for that before we leave?"

The two of them carried along with their conversation, then Marie said, "I'm going to check my office email now," having run out of fishing things she could say.

Jack left to wake Jo up with strict instructions about saying nothing out loud about the upcoming operation. She would feel like a fool whispering in Angela's and her mother's ears, but they were trying to keep things quiet.

They got another knock on the suite door before he used the passkey to enter. Jill handed him a paper with the explanation on it as she walked him over to the sofa. He scanned the note and nodded. They were being listened to, and he was to talk about fishing.

"I'm excited to get out of the city and to the quietness of a lake. Is Nathan planning to cook up our catch?"

It was interesting how each person entering the hotel suite could add something new to a fake fishing expedition.

Jill checked the weather forecast and was happy to see there would be rain later in the day, but not during their supposed trip out on a lake. She wondered when they would be able to resume regular conversations. This was wearing her out. Henrik passed her a note of his own asking, 'I know my technology is secure, and we could use that for texting or emailing. Do you want me to test everyone else's?'

Jill nodded. She would be thrilled to find another way to communicate. She grabbed the cell phones and laptops in the suite and passed them over to Henrik. Unfortunately, Nathan, Jo, and Jack had their phones plugged in for charging in their bedrooms. Angela left her cellphone, and Hope's charging in the kitchen. He disappeared for fifteen minutes and then returned. The technology was secure, but both Jill and Marie had a problem with something on their cell phone covers. He dropped the covers on to some foil and wrapped it up. Henrik determined he could no longer read a signal. He then wiped all the devices clean with a microfiber cloth to make sure they were clear. He brought all of the stuff back to Jill, sending her and Marie texts with the results of his testing. He dropped the foil-wrapped phone covers by the suite door to remind them to take them with them.

Jill begin writing a text for her screen that she would use to tell Angela, Hope, and Nathan about the listening devices when she woke them up. She wasn't sure if they were really going out on a boat with the CIA, so they should dress appropriately. Jill then left to wake the others up. She took her laptop with her where her message was written in large print about the day. It was awkward waking adults up and immediately shoving a laptop screen in their face to read a message, but needs must when the devil drives. Nathan, who was usually the most sluggish of people to wake up, snapped to wakefulness as soon as he read her screen. He was awake, dressed, and in the kitchen in record time, offering to cook breakfast for everyone before their fishing expedition.

When Hope and Angela approached the kitchen attired for a day on the water, Nathan asked if he could get them drink and breakfast.

Hope announced, "I'm going to take my crocheting with me. I'll enjoy watching all of you fish, but I don't want to touch any of those wiggling things."

Marie laughed, "I'm with you, Mom. I'm going to take my laptop, and if the water is smooth enough, I'm going to work on the class I'm teaching this semester at the University. I have papers to grade, and I'd much rather do that than touch slimy things."

Nathan soon had everybody set with a morning beverage of their choice. Their conversation alternated between the fishing expedition, and what they planned to see in their upcoming visit to Montréal. With five minutes to go, they looked around the suite to make sure they would have anything they might need out on the water, as well as their technology. They approached the entrance to the hotel in heavy coats and carrying backpacks or canvas bags with their stuff.

There were two yellow taxis just outside the door with their engines running, and the taxi drivers leaning against the hood.

"Are you the group needing a ride to Rice Lake for a fishing expedition?" he asked.

With those words, they knew that these were the correct taxis. Then Jill had a worried look as she thought that if the Russians were listening, might this be their taxi? The driver correctly interpreted her look, and slightly pulled aside his jacket to reveal a badge that said CIA. She nodded to her team that these were the correct taxis that would take them somewhere safe.

Once they were seated, the taxis left the hotel, and each driver informed its passengers that they would have about an hour's drive to Gore's Landing at Rice Lake, where a boat awaited for their fishing expedition. The atmosphere was tense inside the taxis, as they had had hopes of being able to talk freely in the car, but the taxi drivers passed a note asking them not to discuss anything other than fishing. At least the scenery was pretty, and they now knew they were going to get on an actual boat. Jill watched the driver of her taxi glance in the rearview mirror every few minutes. He was also breaking the law by driving and texting, but the traffic was light in this direction, and so she had no issue.

At one point, he showed his cell phone screen, which revealed that the second driver said there were two cars following them on the highway. Again the tension in the taxis rose higher.

CHAPTER 15

They left Highway 401 and then continued on a country road. They crested a hill and saw the lake before them, dotted with islands in the middle.

"The view is as beautiful as I remember from my time as a child here, I'm sure we'll have a great time fishing on this lake," Jo said.

"Yes, ma'am. This lake has a good reputation for fishing. We have another five minutes, then we'll load on to a boat. You'll all fit on one boat, and there will be a guide or two to help find the right fishing spots. We'll take you inside a building to provide you with any outer-wear that you may need for the cool fall air. The boat that was rented for you also has an interior cabin so that you can get completely out of the weather if need be."

"There are fishing poles there as well?" Jill asked. "This is the lake I used to fish in with my Great Aunt and Uncle."

"Of course. We see that one of your members brought a tackle box, and so we know there are some avid fishermen on this excursion."

Soon they were inside a boat repair building, and they and their technology was scanned. Henrik looked a little affronted as he had already scanned their technology. They removed outerwear and replaced it with jackets provided by their hosts. Once everyone's clothing was changed, and they were not setting off any alarms, they approached the dock to board a cruiser. Their taxi drivers stayed behind, and there were two crew members waiting to hand them aboard.

"Hello, Dr. Quint. I'm agent Tom Simpson with the CIA, welcome aboard. We're going to cast off and head out toward Black Island in the middle of the lake. Thank you all for coming."

"No, thank you, young man, for coming to our rescue. This situation was starting to raise my hair back in Toronto," Hope said.

He chuckled as his other crewmate was showing people around the boat, and pointing out where the bathroom and small galley were. Jack went over to the fishing rods, examining them and selecting one for him and one for Jo. He set his tackle box on the boat deck, and soon they cast off heading for the island in question. Fifteen minutes later, they were behind the island and set anchor for a conversation.

When Hope entered the interior cabin, she'd found Agent Garrett inside. So they had three representatives of the American government on board to assist and protect them.

"Thank you for keeping your cover up until we got to this spot. It couldn't have been easy," said Simpson.

"I'd be the first to admit that from four o'clock this morning to now has been a very stressful time. I don't think any of us are very good at holding false conversations, but clearly you folks had reason to believe we were being bugged, and your scanners at the dock proved you were correct," Jill said. "As always, we're fortunate to have Henrik Klein with our group, as he had the technology to clear our cell phones and laptops so we could at least converse by electronic means. I believe Henrik discovered a tiny transmitter on some cell phone covers, right?"

"I did, and I gave them to the gentleman back at the dock. I didn't think you would want them on this boat. My scanner went off, but I couldn't decipher with my own eyes what they were reacting to, so this must be a tiny transmitter."

"Yes, we've heard rumors that the Russians have been able to develop a new form of listening device. They've managed to instill dust particles with transmitter capabilities, so all they have to do is be close enough to you to throw the dust particles. They will adhere to your clothing, your home, your hair, and your technology."

He saw several members of Jill's team lean over the side of the boat and shake their hair as though to shake loose any dust particles contained therein.

"We know from the scanner that your hair is clean, so no need to worry about that. Either the dust particles didn't land on your hair, or you have since shampooed it and wash them down the drain," Simpson said.

"Whew! I don't like this spy stuff," Hope said. Angela leaned in to give her mom a hug.

"Yes, the covers of some pieces of technology had the dust particles, which is a great way to listen in on phone calls. Jack, thank you for reaching out to your friend Alex Whitehead. Jill, Agent Garrett, also was contacted by the FBI after you reached out to Special Agent Ortiz. We put the story together between our two agencies, and so this is a joint operation."

"Is the Canadian government aware of this operation?" Jill asked, curiously. She liked Detective Ireland and hoped he was in the loop.

"Not yet. We wanted to have a conversation with you first to fully understand the picture. Then Agent Garrett will speak to the Canadians as she is in place as our liaison between our governments."

The other agent aboard was standing guard at the bow of the boat with a pair of powerful binoculars watching boats cross the lake. They hoped they had enough of a head start on the people following them on the highway that they wouldn't have seen where the boat went on the lake. As there were several islands and the lake was twenty-one miles in length, it offered many hiding spots. Unfortunately, they were on a relatively large boat and would stand out for their size alone.

Jill shared her and her team's resume with the CIA official. She discussed their role so far in the murder of the piano player, as well as the shooting in the cemetery from the previous night, and the conclusion of the Toronto police that they couldn't target the Russians that they identified as being physically near them. She ended with their plans to head for Montréal that evening.

Jill smiled when she noticed that Jack was actually fishing. What a way to de-escalate their stress at this moment.

"Jack, are you going to catch and release?"

"No, Nathan said he would make fish and chips for us when we returned to the hotel suite. So I'm catching our late lunch."

"I'll help you," Jo and Angela said together as they grabbed additional fishing rods.

Jill returned to the conversation, grateful for the opportunity to smile. "So we've been contaminated with these dust particles. What should we do with clothing back at the hotel?" Marie asked. "I have the clothes I wore for the last two days in my dirty clothes pillowcase. Should we send out all of the laundry to be washed or dry-cleaned? How about shoes, umbrellas, and purses?"

"When we return to shore, we'll send you back with one of our scanners, and you can determine what to do with your possessions. Certainly, the washing machine will destroy any of them. For other non-washable surfaces, I would take a wet washcloth and clean the surface and re-scan. In the end, you may just have put some pieces in storage until the case is over," replied Simpson.

"I would like to take them back with me to Stuttgart and study the devices, so if any of you find the devices on an item of clothing, please put that item in a bag and give it to me," Henrik said.

The American officers and agent frowned at that, not wanting to give this newly discovered technology away to a German security expert.

"So if I understand this case, the purpose of the pianist and his wife was to assist with Russian spying in the United States and Canada. But, then why would they have the pianist playing in churches? What does that gain you with the listening devices?" Jill asked.

"We haven't figured that out yet. We're not sure the churches were relevant or if their purpose was to re-start the pianist's career."

"Have you looked at the congregations?" Hope asked. "Maybe it's more about the people in these churches than music."

Agent Simpson was impressed with her question. He'd thought she was just the crocheting mother of one of the pathologist's team members, but her question was quite insightful.

"That's an excellent question, and the very one we asked ourselves and Anna Chernov."

"So, you know where she is?" Jill asked, happy to hear she might be alive.

"Yes, she defected to a Chicago Police station. She brought a sample of the dust particle with her and insisted that the police call the FBI. She came with a note written in English, but she did not speak the language, and so we had to find a Russian interpreter within our agencies to interview her."

"Does she know her husband is dead?" asked Marie.

"She does now. He was murdered after she was in our protection for a couple days. She asked that we make arrangements for him to be buried in the United States, as she knew she would never return to Russia. We have agency personnel meeting with the Toronto medical examiner so his remains can be moved to an as yet to be determined location in the US. She is grieving her husband, and she is pregnant, but the couple had known and planned for her defection, and knew that his death might be a likely consequence of action."

"That is so sad," Hope said. "Let us say a prayer for Anna Chernov and her future baby."

Jill nodded solemnly at Hope's words and said, "Did she supply the reason for his church performances?"

"No. They were told the churches were prominent, and that would boost Nikita's reputation in his return to the piano world."

"Did she say anything about his parents? We observed payment to them as well as apartment leases from the agent of the pianist."

"We didn't ask her that question, nor did we find that in our research yet. You're one step ahead of us, Dr. Quint."

"My colleague Jo is brilliant at following the trail of money even in a foreign language and in an accounting system that's very different from the US. You should make her a job offer, she would be quite an asset to either of your agencies, although my investigations would suffer her loss, so I've changed my mind, don't make her a job offer," Jill said grinning.

"I heard that, and I have a good job already thank you very much," Jo called out from the boat's railing.

They heard a buzzing coming from somewhere in the sky above, and their lookout looked into the distance to see a drone flying about the lake.

The agent on watch said, "Simpson, I believe that drone is for us. Should we shoot it out of the sky?"

Agent Garrett and Officer Simpson conferred. Firing a weapon in Canada came with consequences. Was anyone enough of a marksman to take out the drone? Might the drone be armed?

"Could you throw this sweater I'm crocheting on the drone? The weave would get in the way of the propellers," Hope suggested.

Jill's entire team just grinned at the suggestion. They loved nonviolent ways to take something or someone out.

"That's an interesting suggestion," Simpson said as he called out to the officer on watch to determine if the drone was armed with any weapons.

The answer came back that it was not armed.

"Okay then, we're going to have to have a reason for the drone to get very close to the boat, and then we need someone to hide and throw the sweater over it before it can be moved. You folks fishing need to come inside the cabin. That should get the drone close enough so that it has to confirm that you ladies are the people it's searching for," Simpson said, directing the officer to take cover underneath a canvas roof that was laying on the boat's floor in case it rained. Hope quickly tied off the yarn she was using to crochet and passed the sweater to the officer. They all huddled just inside the open doorway of the cabin and watched the drone approach the boat.

"You're sure this thing isn't armed? It looks bigger than the average drone," Jill said. "I use one for my winery back in California. It's a great way to look at acres of vines while sitting at a computer screen."

"I think it's bigger because it's a longer-range drone, but I've never seen one that shape be able to fire weapons. Besides, those types of drones are not for sale in the United States or Canada, and I doubt you could ship such a device through customs."

Jill's team waited nervously as the drone approached, hoping the CIA officer knew his drones. Jill was amazed at the arrogance of the drone operator to get it so close to the people on the boat. She could see a single eyeball peeking out from the canvas cover and crossed her fingers that his timing would be exquisite. She sensed everybody hold their breath at the same moment with the hope that the sweater would work to disable the propellers. The agent sprung out with the sweater and managed to catch one of the propellers, which was enough to bring the entire drone down.

"I know technology, I can disconnect the remote control of this device by removing the battery," Henrik said, approaching the officer holding the drone, while the remote operator continued to try to get it out of the clutches of the sweater. He reached in and quickly pulled open the latch containing the batteries, and just like that, the movement ceased.

Jack whispered, "Henrik, how about the camera; does it have a separate battery?"

"We're good. The battery that flies the drone also powers the camera. Now I suggest we move this boat to another location, as I'm sure we were detected before we brought the drone down. Who knows if they have a second drone coming our way."

They could hear boats on the lake, but they were all too distant to worry about them.

"Henrik is right, they used a Mosin 54 mm rifle against us in the cemetery, and that's a Russian sniper rifle. So they don't have to get that close, though we're helped by the waves hitting both their boat and ours."

The officers and agents discussed where to move the boat, knowing there was a potential sniper on the lake with them.

"We could make a run for one of the two rivers that empty from this lake. Forty miles one way puts us in Lake Ontario and New York, or twenty miles in the other direction will put us in the city of Peterborough, which has an airport. We could also stay in the middle of the lake where the waves are the biggest, or head for one of the cities on the lake. We would be vulnerable if their boat got close to this boat as we approached the shore."

"Your agencies should have taken control of the Russians before we got on the boat. We knew they were following from Toronto to here," Nathan said, not liking that they were sitting ducks in the potential range of a sniper.

"We didn't bring enough assets with us to do that," replied Simpson. "I see we greatly underestimated our foes."

Henrik had been looking at the map and was unimpressed with the two agencies. They were going to get them killed if they continued to underestimate their enemy.

"Let's go now and head to the Otonabee River. The river has some open areas, but I can have my plane meet us at Peterborough airport if we can survive the river and ditch the boat. The plane will hold all of us," he said, pulling up the anchor and putting the boat in full throttle heading toward the river inlet.

Jill approached him and said, "Thanks for taking control."

Henrik nodded and dialed his pilot to get his plane moved from Toronto City Airport to Peterborough.

"Are you going to get some help for us?" Hope asked of the officers.

Simpson had been on the phone and looked chagrined. "There are no resources within two hours of here without calling the Canadian Police. As this is not an authorized operation. We have some explaining to do, so we're on our own until the right diplomatic lines have been established."

"Why don't I call Detective Ireland? Diplomacy aside, we'd like to live another day, and we have a Russian assassin on our tail. As a private citizen, you can't order me not to do that, and you can tell your superiors that I said that," Jill said, hitting the speed dial button for Detective Ireland. Jill moved away from Simpson in case he was tempted to grab her phone, but he probably secretly agreed with her idea. She noted Henrik wave at her and she hit the end button on her phone to hear what he had to say.

Henrik waved at her, pointing to the map, as she waited for Detective Ireland to answer. "There's a Canadian Coast Guard Station not far from here in Quinte West, perhaps your detective can marshal resources from there?"

Jill looked at the map and agreed with Henrik's suggestion. Meanwhile, she noticed that both the FBI agent and the CIA officer were working their channels, while the other officer sat down on the highest level of the boat with binoculars searching for the enemy boat. Nathan meanwhile was checking boat rentals around the lake to see who rented a larger horsepower than their boat.

"I checked the boat rentals around the lake, and no one has

boats for rent with greater horsepower than ours, but we are weighted down by the number of people aboard this boat."

Everyone nodded at that analysis and looked around for a place to offload weight, but decided that would likely ruin their head start.

This time Jill connected the call to Detective Ireland, "Yes, Dr. Quint?

"We've got a problem and need your help."

"It's rather early in the morning for you to be in trouble again. Has your shooter from last night found you again, and if so, where are you?"

"There are eleven of us on a boat on Rice Lake. We're heading for the Otonabee River, but we sure could use some help from the nearby Coast Guard Base at Quinte West. We just downed a drone that we think was likely from the Russians as we believe they followed us here this morning."

She decided she would leave off the part about the CIA and FBI.

"There's a long story behind your explanation, but I've learned you don't exaggerate. Can you describe the boat you're on, and give me your Geo-coordinates at the moment and I understand you're heading toward the river."

"It's a white and gray cruiser style boat with an interior cabin." She looked at her cell phone and pressed the buttons for coordinates. "We can see the mouth of the river, and our coordinates are 44.148064, -78.228960."

She didn't need to say that they would be different by the time any aid reached them. She heard a sound and ducked.

"Okay, we're officially under fire. We just heard a gunshot, so hurry, please."

"Will do." and the call ended.

Jill looked behind their boat to see where the shots came from, and they saw a pontoon boat slowly gaining ground on them.

"Do we have any protection we can put over the engines? If they get shot, we die."

The agent and officer sacrificed their protective wear, and they strapped the vests around the engines.

Henrik was swerving erratically, trying to reduce the possibility of an accurate shot but still keeping their forward progress to the maximum. The curve of the river would offer some coverage at the beginning, but then there was a straight stretch where they would be vulnerable.

Jill checked her watch, knowing that if the detective was able to scramble air resources, it would take a minimum of ten minutes to convince anyone to work on their behalf and perhaps fifteen minutes to reach them by air.

"Can your plane do anything?" Jill asked Henrik, knowing it was in the air.

"Not really. I would be afraid to buzz the Russians for fear that they would get a shot in. I could dump fuel on them, but I would damage the lake or river doing so, and my pilots might miss. Maybe if I take another vacation with you, I'll add some amenities to the plane," Henrik said, smiling.

"You're enjoying this, aren't you?" Jill asked.

"I think I've said it in the past, it's never a dull day with you around Jill. Also, I go home with ideas in my head of how to better protect people in non-violent ways, so you're good for my business."

"Even if she doesn't take your marketing job?" Marie said from his other side, her arm slung around his shoulder. Angela, Jack, Jo, and Hope were in the cabin. Marie had been there too, but she was too antsy to stay while they were being chased.

Jill's cell phone vibrated. She didn't recognize the number, but it was coming from Toronto.

"Hello."

"Dr. Quint, this is Detective Chloe Kim. I'm going to stay on the phone with you and let you know what's going on on our end.

We have multiple resources on their way to you. We have the Ontario Provincial Police on some access roads close to the river. They will be unable to do anything more than use a PA speaker to yell at the boat. As you follow the river, the first bridge you come to is the Bensfort bridge. We have Provincial Police stationed on that bridge to provide you with protection. They have a variety of weapons that they can use for any boat chasing you. You just have to get there. We were also able to marshal a helicopter from the Trenton Air Force Base. It will reach the lake in about ten minutes. Where are you at the moment? Who is driving your boat, and who is on board?"

Jill thought she heard background noise behind the detective and wondered if she was in some kind of command center.

"We've left the lake and we're on the river. You've met most of my team. Henrik is driving the boat, Marie, Nathan, and I are standing on the bridge with him. Angela, Jo, Jack, and Hope are in the cabin. We also have Agent Garrett from the FBI aboard, with two other officers."

Jill thought that the CIA would hate to be caught on this boat without notification to Canadian authorities. And perhaps they would assume the other two 'officers' were from the FBI. But if they were going to get blown to bits at some point by the Russians chasing them, the police should know precisely how many people they needed to recover. Then she decided she needed to dump her morbid thoughts and concentrate on helping them survive, rather than planning their dead body recovery.

She heard the detective relaying the news of who was on board the boat to whoever was in the room with her, and then she asked, "Can you see the boat chasing you?"

Jill looked back, and so far, the river was clear.

"No, and there have been no further gunshots. I wonder if they decided not to follow us into the river as there would be limited options for them to escape the Canadian Police."

"That's good news. Do you have a description of the boat? If you don't need defense from the air, perhaps they can look for the men chasing you."

"Just a moment."

Jill put her phone on hold and then went to talk to Simpson, who was kneeling at the stern of the boat. Jill still didn't see the chase boat but thought it best to kneel in case they came into range. It was noisy next to the motors and with the wind.

"Do you have a description of the boat chasing us?"

"Not much that will help. It was a white and silver pontoon boat, which is to say it looks like just about every other pontoon boat on the lake. There were two men on board. They've disappeared since we entered the river, so hopefully, we're good. What's our status on help?"

"There's a bridge up ahead that has Provincial Police in position, and the Air Force base at Trenton has sent a helicopter to our aid. Henrik's plane is en route to a local airport, so we'll be dumping this boat at that point. There's room for you on the plane, but someone needs to return this boat to Gore's Landing."

Simpson looked impressed and said, "I think we need to hire you at the CIA to run our operations. You've marshaled resources quickly."

"Yeah, well, you better talk to Agent Garrett and work on your story. I was asked who was on board this boat. I said, 'Agent Garrett and two officers. I didn't say you were two officers from the CIA, so that's for you to work out with her," Jill returned to her position next to Henrik, and reconnected to Detective Kim.

"The boat description won't help you much. It's white and silver like every other pontoon boat out here. There were two men aboard. Our folks at the boat's stern haven't seen the boat since we entered the river."

"That continues to be good news. I'll ask the helicopter to reach you on the river, then head back toward the lake to look for the boat. Did you get a look at the gun the Russians used?"

Again Jill put the detective on hold and approached Simpson, she still didn't see a boat behind them, so this time she just bent to ask him, "Did you see the weapon the Russians were using?"

"It was a sniper rifle with a suppressor on it, but I couldn't tell you the make or model."

"How do you know there was a suppressor on it? It sounded pretty loud to me."

"The suppressor decreases the sound, it doesn't eliminate it. There was no muzzle flash, and a suppressor eliminates that."

"Okay," Jill replied, filing that comment away for future reference. She took her phone off hold and relayed the information to the detective.

She looked back, and still, no one had entered the river behind them. Then she heard a helicopter in the distance and could see it flying towards them. Jill relayed that information, and they watched as the beast thundered over them and toward the mouth of the river. She hoped it would catch the Russians on the lake.

"Are we going too fast in the river?" Jill asked Henrik, looking at the wake their boat was making.

"We've been exceeding the limit, but there's no one else in the river at the moment, and I think we would get a pass this once. Remember, Canadians are known for being nice."

Jill smiled at Marie and at a smirking Henrik.

"It's nice when you have the humor to handle a stressful situation. I'm going to tell the others they can come out of the cabin if they want as we appear to be safe at the moment."

She knew her opinion was correct when she saw Garrett and Simpson removing the protective vests from the motors and putting them back on. Everyone assembled on the boat deck happy to be breathing fresh air even though it was the brisk variety of fall. She saw Hope say something to Henrik and pat him on the back.

Jill was so relieved now that they appeared to be out of danger, that she forgot her phone was open to Detective Kim. She raised it to her ear to see if the detective was still there.

"Hello?"

"Any more sightings of the shooter?" came the detective's question confirming she was still on the other end of the call.

"No sightings of them. They must've weighed the positives of killing us on the river versus being cornered by law enforcement in the narrow passage. The helicopter flew over us and went towards the lake. Have they found the boat?"

"They did a brief survey of the few boats on the lake, but none of them contained just two men, so they have returned to base. Do you see the bridge in the distance yet?"

"We just entered the horseshoe of the river, and once we make this curve, according to our map, we should be able to see the bridge in the distance. With the curve in the river, our visibility has been reduced to see who is behind us. If no one is, then I think you can pull your officers off the bridge, and we'll continue to the Peterborough Airport where Henrik's plane will take us back to Toronto."

"You Americans seem to live a fantasy life," said the detective with attitude in her voice.

"Right now, I would trade that fantasy life and walk back to Toronto, if that's what it took to get an assassin off our back. Remember, this all started while we were on vacation in your beautiful country, just trying to listen to classical music. Now, we've had two murder attempts on our lives. I think once we land in Toronto, we will pack our bags and head to Montréal. Hopefully, the Russians won't follow us there, and we would appreciate it if you would pass on to law enforcement there that our stories are legitimate. When we call for help, we mean it."

"We need to get a report from you before you leave. We mobilized significant resources to come to your aid, set up a command post, and worried as to whether you would survive your boat ride. We need more than just a 'thanks' on a cell phone. We'll be at your hotel when you arrive," the detective said, abruptly ending the call.

Jill briefly looked at her cell phone and said to no one in

particular, "I think I've just been hung upon. The police will be at the hotel when we return and want to talk to us. Agent Simpson, will you and your second mate there be returning with us?"

"Yes, I'm afraid you can run, but you can't hide. If I know my Russian operatives, they will hunt you down until they can kill you. Sometimes it takes years, but it could be in just a few days in Montréal."

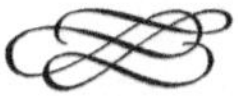

The remainder of the boat ride was uneventful, and the Provincial Police must have been told to assist the Americans. They got off the boat at the bridge, made arrangements to get the boat back to Gore's Landing, and rode in the police cars to the airport. They were back in less than two hours after the first shots were fired.

When they arrived at the hotel, they were greeted by Hassan, Ireland, Kim, and someone new.

"This is Officer Bell from the Canadian Security Intelligence Agency," Hassan said. "I don't believe we met everyone in your party, Dr. Quint."

There was anger and suspicion in his voice with this last statement.

Simpson stepped forward and made the introductions for his agency.

Jill's temper was starting to boil. Nathan, an expert in cooking, sensed the pot about to boil over. He thought about trying to turn down the heat under that pot, but sometimes it was good for outsiders to be burned as the water overflowed.

"Look, all of you," Jill said, waving her hand at the various law enforcement agency representatives from both countries, "can take your disparaging attitudes and leave," pointing to the hotel's door. "My team has not caused the situation. When being shot at, we've asked for police protection and nothing more out of the lot of you. We came close to dying in a cemetery last night and again today out on a lake. All of you are underestimating the Russians. You all have your secrets that you're keeping from us, and that's affecting our safety. We're going to go upstairs and pack our bags and leave for Montréal. You can warn the next province of the issues here if you care to, but most of all, take your attitude and get out of my sight!"

Nathan thought he had never seen Jill this enraged. He suspected, in part, it was due to Hope's presence. It was bad enough when Jill's team was endangered, but for that danger to encompass the honorary mother of her team, and then for the various law enforcement types to view her with suspicion and not share information, prompted her to act with such rudeness.

Henrik also understood the situation and stepped in to fan additional flames at the law enforcement group.

With his arm around Marie, he said, "We're going to return to our suite and pack our bags. Agent Simpson, if we can borrow your listening device sensor, we'll wrap all of our contaminated clothing and objects with foil and be careful with our conversations. My plane is being readied for a trip to Montréal. I've ordered our transportation to the airport. Shall we meet at the hotel entrance in an hour? Is that enough time for everyone to decompress and pack their bags?"

Jo liked to play peacemaker and so said, "Yes, that's plenty of time. If Nathan pours all of us a glass of wine or better still make a Bloody Mary, we can take that to our bedrooms, pack and decompress at the same time."

Agent Garrett was perhaps the best bridge between the two countries and four agencies and so said, "Why don't we find a room where we can chat about this incident and our plan for going forward with the Russians? I was on the boat today and can relay any information about that incident."

Detective-Sargent Hassan hadn't become the leader of the detective division by being slow to read people's emotions and actions. He knew the best step he could take to get a handle on the case was to follow the FBI agent's suggestion. This was his city to protect, and he didn't like that he didn't have a response to the American doctor's disgust with how this case was being handled.

At the sound of the elevator door opening, Jill and her crew boarded for the short ride to their suite. The door closed on the agents who were still dumbstruck by Jill's outburst. Nathan was the first to speak after the elevator doors closed. "Well done, babe," as he leaned into to kiss Jill. His words touched her soul and made her eyes water as the tension that had been building since the call from the CIA at four that morning began to dissipate. It has been a stressful twenty-four hours and they weren't out of the woods, yet, but they were all still alive and together.

As they were wont to do, they formed in for a tight circle and group hug.

"Thanks, guys," Jill mumbled, trying to get her emotions under control.

They stayed together awhile longer until the elevator arrived on their floor then Nathan broke them up with a lighthearted, "Okay, friends, I'll get the libation of choice for everyone. Time to drink and pack," he said, opening the door to the suite and entering the kitchen to open a bottle of wine and then to pour the ingredients of Jo and Marie's Bloody Mary into a blender.

They each grabbed a glass and headed for their rooms to pack. Jill threw her arms around Nathan, and gave a watery mumble, "They all nearly died today on the boat and what do they do, but give me a hug. I'm honored to have such loyal and true friends, and I think I might need two glasses of wine to get my emotions under control.

Nathan looked at his watch and whispered, "Let's quickly

pack, then take a few minutes to ourselves before we leave to go meet Henrik's transportation. Okay?"

At the designated time, they all left the suite to head downstairs with their luggage. With the aid of Officer Simpson's gadget, they were assured that there were no listening devices that weren't shielded from listening. Nathan used the hotel-provided laundry bag to carry out the liquor he'd acquired in Toronto. As they walked through the lobby, Hassan called out to Jill just before she reached the door. There was a stretch limo waiting to take them to the city airport.

"Is there room for us to join you?" Hassan asked Jill.

"I don't know. Ask Henrik. Someone will have to fetch you back from the City airport."

Jill saw Hassan conversing with Henrik, and soon he, Officer Simpson, Agent Garrett, and officer Bell, joined them in the limo. City airport was close to downtown, so the ride would last only about twenty minutes before they boarded a ferry that would cross the short water distance to the airport. Once there, a private aviation gate would take them to Henrik's plane.

As they set off, Hassan started by offering an apology to Jill for his lack of faith in her investigative skills. Detectives Ireland and Kim were working with a multi-agency task force that was being set up. The Montréal Police and the Sûreté du Québec were members as well so Jill and team would have protection there.

Wow, thought Jill, Agent Garrett or Officer Simpson had created an amazing turnaround in attitude from the Detective-Sargeant. There was nothing like being shot at to motivate you to change your perspective and that of your fellow police officers.

"That's good news. Did you round up the men surveilling our hotel in Toronto?" Jill tested the Detective-Sargeant's change of attitude.

"We planned to if they were there, but they must have all followed you to the lake and haven't made it back into position yet. Hopefully, they'll be unable to follow you to Montréal. We had your hotel list your next hotel as one in St. John's, Newfoundland. Your Russians will waste a lot of time searching for you there. The RCMP will be on the lookout for any activity in that city."

"Excellent. Perhaps, we'll have a peaceful vacation in the Province of Québec. Was there any trace of the men at Rice Lake? Did the Ontario Provincial Police find any evidence of their visit?"

"They abandoned their boat at a public dock at Pinecrest. They must have had their driver meet them there as it's not far from Gore's Landing. It took an hour or two for someone to notice that the boat had been abandoned and to take a look at it. It was stamped with Harris Boats Works information, and so they were notified that the boat was there, and they called the OPP. They provided us with the identity of the man who rented the boat. He paid cash and placed a phony credit card on it. They used a fake Ontario driver's license. Our crime scene team is en route now, but they were probably smart enough, and it was cold enough to wear gloves."

"Yes, but perhaps there's a shell casing that rolled into the boat that they didn't pick up. I would also look for fingerprints near the front of the boat as most snipers like their fingers bare for firing a gun."

"Fingerprints are iffy. Per the boat rental, they wipe down the boats with bleach after each rental, but still, I'm not hopeful for any evidence collection from the boat. We could have hundreds of innocent fingerprints on that boat."

"So is your department going to solve this homicide? You have a lot of clues here in Toronto and from the information given by the wife. Will you be looking at Russians now?"

Hassan sighed, "Yes. Officer Bell will be interviewing the Philharmonic Conductor, and the others you identified as soon as we get back to our division."

"Good. It wasn't like I was asking you to interview your entire Russian population here in Toronto. Rather there were just five or six people I wanted the police to have a conversation with. We now know that mother Russia is behind this murder and the further attempts on our lives. Perhaps, you should just announce it on the news, and that will make the Russians fold and go home."

"Actually, we think that you have become a twofer as I believe you Americans call it – a two for one. I understand you've prevailed in the arrest of other Russians in some of your past cases, and that has come to the attention of whoever is pulling the strings in Moscow. They kill you, and they think they end the piano player murder investigation, and they take care of someone who has been an ongoing source of pain. We would be happy to see you get on a plane and head home to California for the safety of Canada, you understand?"

Jill had heard this song before, 'Please go home and take the violence bubble with you' jingle. She gave Hassan a slight smile and said, "You've talked to your counterparts in the United States, haven't you? I try to protect my local Sheriff from the occupational hazards of my job, and so you need to arrest some people before I leave Canada."

"I'll be joining you in Montréal, and I would appreciate notification of your hotel address before you leave," Officer Garrett said.

Jill opened her mouth to reply to the agent and Henrik talked over her, "Excuse me Jill, but I've found that I can enjoy more of your company if you stay close by me."

Jill cut in, having an inkling of where the conversation was going and said, "So you've canceled your fancy hotel and you're joining us at our two-star hotel?"

"No, I love your company, but not enough to make that kind of a sacrifice. I've booked the entire group into a house. It has eight bedrooms, a kitchen for Nathan, a dining room, a living room with space for murder boards for Jill, a first-level bedroom for Hope, and it's adjacent to a park with running trails for Marie. My company is there now installing security. We'll be safe there, and not have to worry about talkative hotel staff. Here's the address Detective-Sargent if you want to pass it on to your Québec counterparts," Henrik said passing a slip of paper over to Hassan.

Jill took a few seconds to think about how she felt about Henrik's heavy-handed tactics. In the end, she decided that they would likely be safer in such a location, and so it was a good idea.

"Can we pay for our share of the bill?" Angela asked.

Henrik looked a little chagrinned and said, "It's actually cheaper than the bill for my suite at the Empress Hotel in downtown, so I'm saving money."

Marie looked up the property after Henrik had given her the address and said, "This looks very nice and it has so many amenities we won't need to step outside, but I for one, want to tour Montréal!"

There were thanks to Henrik around the car, and the various law enforcement representatives moved onto their plans for finding the Russians.

"Agent Garrett informed us that you were followed from your hotel this morning and that men had the hotel under surveillance. I believe that you didn't pass that information onto Detective Ireland as you thought we wouldn't be receptive to it. I'm sorry that we created that impression, and I'm glad Mr. Klein is installing additional security at your residence in Montréal. I believe you identified some of the men in front of your hotel?"

"Yes. It was again our Mr. Tamm and a new person which we only partially identified as Sergey Shishin. We haven't caught his full face on video, so we're only eighty percent sure it's him."

"Do you think there are more men than the two you've identified?" Garrett asked.

"Logically, yes. If one guy stayed with the car and two went with the boat, than that makes three. Besides, who would be able to stay awake for twenty-hours on surveillance of our hotel? It's such a boring assignment, to be effective, you would need to rotate off of it. I have to think there are a lot of Russians spies in

North America. Maybe the guy called in additional help when it seemed that things were heating up here in Canada. Surely, that's the way the CIA works?" Jill asked of Simpson.

"I can neither confirm nor deny that statement," Officer Simpson said.

"You sound like a talking head at a press conference," Marie said.

"You have to memorize that phrase to graduate from CIA school," Simpson said with a slight smile.

"So we should be safe in Montréal, right?" asked Nathan.

"Depends on whether we're being followed now to the airport, or if they know the wing number of the airplane, or if any of us mentioned that we were going there while the listening devices were planted on our clothing. I think there's a good chance we will be followed there. We may be hard to locate since we're staying at a private home, but it would be our dumb luck to trip over the men at a tourist location," Jill replied.

"So maybe we should stay at distilleries, wineries, and breweries as they are rarely on the top of anyone's top ten 'must-dos' in Montréal."

Of course, Nathan would suggest that.

"That's a thought to avoid the Russians. We should look up the top attractions and stay away from any of them that would allow a shooter to take aim."

"That's a grim thought, Jill. We have led blessed lives and will continue to do so. Let's not worry about the Russians and see what we want to see. I doubt I'll ever be in Montréal again, so we need to see some of my favorites," Hope said.

Everyone agreed with Hope, because how could they not?

The limousine pulled up to the plane and they all looked in awe of the large private jet in front of them. Hope was right, they were very fortunate to be living these lives.

"I've had a staff person looking out for anyone watching the plane or following the limo as we approached the entrance,"

Henrik said pointing to someone just inside the plane holding binoculars.

The group looked around for someone who didn't belong even though they didn't know what that person necessarily looked like. Then they began loading their luggage into the cargo area of the jet and climbed aboard. It would be a short flight – a little more than an hour, but with no security screening or waiting for other passengers to board, it almost didn't feel like they were flying at all.

The attendant continued with surveillance of the airfield and across the narrow swath of water to the waterfront sidewalk. She called Henrik over to view something she saw through the binoculars.

"Our Mr. Tamm or whatever his name is has followed us to this location. It shouldn't be too difficult to find out where we're going," Henrik said to the cabin at large.

Jill pulled out her cell and dialed Detective-Sargent Hassan to pass on the sighting of their Russian assassin.

CHAPTER 17

Andrei Danilov was having an incredibly bad day. Moscow had called him at the ungodly hour of four in the morning to tell him that the listening devices revealed that the Americans were going fishing at a nearby lake that morning and it was a perfect location to kill them on the water. His assignment had changed from watching and then executing a piano player, to killing this enemy of Russia, Dr. Quint. Ha, what did Moscow know? He'd paid the doorman at the American's hotel, and found that they were going fishing on Rice Lake. Andrei didn't know where they were going in the lake until he heard Gore's Landing along the way. When he'd first heard about the lake, he noted there were several places that someone could rent a boat, and so he'd had to follow them to the lake to know where they might be on the lake.

The Americans had left their personal belongings behind at the wharf. So they'd been unable to hear their conversation aboard their boat. He had one of men follow the boat with binoculars, while he rented a boat from a different nearby marina. He and Sergey pulled their rifles out of their trunk and headed out behind the other boat about fifteen minutes later. Alexey stayed on the shore watching the boats recede from his higher vantage point.

He and Sergey followed the boat behind the island, put their boat in neutral and looked at the people through their scopes to confirm it was the Americans. To confirm these were indeed the Americans they were looking for, they launched a drone for a closer look. Much to their chagrin, the Americans captured the drone and Sergey couldn't get it back out of the American hands.

Another boat was trolling for fish nearby, and they had to wait for it to pass out of range. They had suppressors on the rifle, but the guns still made a lot of noise when fired. While they waited, the American boat, which had been at anchor, suddenly took off in full power. It didn't head for shore and it had been a quick decision to go, as there were a couple of people fishing who had to pull their rods up quickly. He and Sergey kneeled at the front of their boat, aiming at the fleeing boat, but just as they squeezed the trigger, a wave hit their boat. They muttered a few expletives, then put the rifles in the bottom of the boat and took off after the Americans. They began gaining ground on the Americans, with Sergey driving the boat, while he was studying the map of the lake to determine where the Americans might be going.

"I think they're headed to the river."

"Let's see if we can catch them before they get there. We have poor aim from this boat, though. This bouncing on the waves is too much for me to get a shot off. Once we get close to the shore, the water will be smoother. Maybe we can aim for the motors on the back of the boat. If we kill their power, they'll be dead in the water in more ways than one," Sergey said.

They took one more shot and missed, and they could see the mouth of the river. There was a long stretch of river in front of them, but it would be too easy to get pinned downed by Canadian authorities if they went there.

"Let's turn around and dump this boat here," Andrei said,

pointing to a city called Pinecrest. "I'm going to call Alexey, and have him meet us there with the car."

They were nearly back at their intended dock when they saw a helicopter appear in the distance about where they thought the river was. It briefly flew over boats in the lake, and then lifted and disappeared to wherever it came from.

"Good call Andrei. Had we not pulled anchor when we did , we might be in the custody of the Canadians right now."

They tied the boat up to the public dock, grabbed their rifle cases and walked uphill to where their car was waiting. Alexey was using binoculars to keep the area under surveillance.

"What are you going to do with the boat?" he asked.

"I thought about pulling some wires off the motor and claiming it was disabled, but after seeing the helicopter, I know the authorities were called in to aid the Americans, and so know we were on that lake in a boat, so there's no reason to try and hide our presence. Eventually, someone will notice that the boat's been abandoned at that dock and will call it in, but there's no reason to make it easy."

"Where to now, Andrei?" Alexey asked.

"We head back to Toronto and resume our surveillance of the hotel. The Americans will need to return at some point, and it's just a matter of having another opportunity to kill this Dr. Quint."

"Are we able to listen to their conversations?"

"Not according to Moscow. They aren't sure if they discovered the devices or changed clothing. They mentioned at one point that they were leaving for Montréal this evening, so we need to watch the hotel for when they leave with luggage. I assume they're taking a plane, but perhaps it's a train. We also know they observed us sitting in the car outside of the hotel. So Alexey, I think we need to place you across the street in a café. We heard that they had identified me and many of my identities, and they have mostly identified Sergey. Still, they don't know who you are. Rather than place you in a car on a street which seems to be under surveillance by the hotel's cameras, I thought it would be a better idea to seat you in the café at the window so you can watch from there. Sergey and I will be around the corner, ready in a car, when the Americans leave the hotel. There should be time to pick you up as it will take some time to load their luggage and the people in cars."

"If they already know that we're surveilling them, why try to make it a secret? We could just sit in our cars around the hotel," Sergey said.

"I'm afraid they might have convinced the police that we're a threat. If the police pulled us over and found the sniper rifles in the trunk, we would not escape their clutches. We need to be stealthy about this," Andrei replied.

"We're going to have to go home to Russia permanently after we kill the Americans. They know a little too much about us for us to stay in North America," Sergey said. "I've grown to like it here. There's plenty of vodka, good food, and it's much warmer than home. Maybe my next assignment can be somewhere warm."

"Be careful what you wish for. You could be sent to Cuba, which is warm, but not as comfortable as here. You would be sunburned the first year you spend in Cuba, and hiding weapons isn't easy when it's too hot to wear a lot of clothing," Alexey advised.

The three men acknowledged that thought as he approached the tall buildings of Toronto.

"Let's at least turn this car in and get a new one. No sense in making it easy for the police to locate us," Andrei said.

They detoured to change cars and collect their meager belongings from the hotel room they shared. They hardly spent any time there trying to keep track of the Americans. This assignment continued to get worse every day despite the decent climate, incredible food, and large city to hide in. It should have been easy to kill the piano player, then return to the embassy in New York City, and await their next assignment in relative comfort. It was depressing to know that they might fail at this assignment and certainly never again enjoy the lifestyle of North America. There was also an edge that things could get a lot worse quickly, either in the form of an American or Canadian jail or perhaps in a worse location like a Siberian coal mine. They needed to complete this assignment and then get some help getting out of the country to anywhere else, otherwise it might take weeks to take the rail across Canada, walk over the border into Alaska, and lay low there until mid-summer when they could take a boat into Russian territory. It was better than being arrested and interrogated, but not by much. It would be a long, cold, and dangerous journey.

They had a sense of urgency that had been absent up to this point in what had seemed to be a routine mission. Andrei and Sergey dropped Alexey off at the café and found a parking space two blocks away and out of the camera range of the hotel. They settled in the respective locations, prepared to wait for hours for the Americans to depart. Alexey was surprised when in less than an hour, he saw a large limousine arrive.

He said into his phone, "I think the Americans are leaving. A large limousine has pulled up to the hotel."

"Do you see the Americans?"

"Not yet. The vehicle is huge, and I can't imagine it's for anyone other than that large group."

There was silence on the phone while Alexey watched, and Andrei and Sergey prepared to swoop in and pick up Alexey to tail the large vehicle.

"Okay, they just appeared at the hotel doors. I'll meet you at the curb," Alexey said and disconnected the phone. He left the café and approached the curb, keeping his face down and the hood on his jacket covering his head. He didn't want to be identified by the authorities like his comrades had. With their cover blown, they had to leave. He was still safe to stay and work and preferred to do so.

When the car arrived at the curb, he got in, and they continued down the street to make a U-turn, so they were facing the same direction as the limo. Sergey was looking through binoculars and said, "I think some law enforcement types are riding with them. I wish we could just shoot a rocket at them and blow the car up along with the passengers."

"We haven't been able to buy one on the black market, so forget that solution."

Within a few minutes, they were on the move.

"They're not heading for the Toronto airport. They would've made a right turn and got on the freeway. The train station is behind us, as is the freeway to Montréal. It's too far for a helicopter ride. I wonder where they're going?" Andrei said.

Sergey removed the binoculars from his eyes and looked down at the map on his phone and said, "I think they're heading to the Billy Bishop City Airport. Let me google the airport; it looks like it's on an island."

After a few seconds of searching, he said, "We can park the car and take a nine-hundred-foot pedestrian tunnel over to the airport. They are probably taking a ferry across. They can just stay in the limousine, and it takes less than two minutes. This is like the river, if we cross over to the airport island, our means of escape will be limited."

"So, we just watch them leave?" Alexey said with frustration in his voice.

"The stakes are too high for us at this location. I'm going to find a place to view that airport, and one of us should cross the pedestrian bridge to see which plane they get on. Follow them into the terminal and listen to where their bags get checked." Andrei told Alexey as they stopped at the passenger loading zone.

Alexey started towards the pedestrian tunnel leading to the airport. At the same time, Sergey and Andrei parked their car and walked along the waterfront, looking for a vantage point to view the island. Using the binoculars, they scoped the airport which consisted of commercial jets and private planes. All Andrei wanted to do was confirm that the Americans were heading for Montréal, then he would call Alexey back, and they would leave for Montréal. It was over a five-hour drive, but they could not risk trying to get through airport security.

Sergey was looking through binoculars and saw the limo cross an airport road heading to a private plane.

"There's their limo, they're taking a private plane."

"Can you read the numbers on their wing? We can track where the plane is going. I'm going to call Alexey back as he can't see anything inside the airport."

Sergey changed his position, and the focus on his binoculars until he could see the tail number.

Andrei finished his call with Alexey and said, "Let's head for Montréal now. The plane will be in the air in about fifteen minutes, and we can view it on this software to see where it's going to confirm that it's Montréal. If it's not, we'll have to devise a new plan to find the Americans."

"How will we find them in Montréal? We won't be there to track where they go after their plane lands. Also, there are two airports there, so if we were in town, we'd need to track both of them," Sergey asked.

"I asked for more resources, and there's a Consulate in Montréal that is going to send people to watch the two airports and follow the Americans to their hotel."

"Good."

They reached the car and waved over Alexey. Andrei threw the keys to him, and they piled into the car. As they left the parking lot, they heard sirens coming toward them.

"I wonder if the Americans spotted us, and those sirens are for us? When I was looking for the tail number, I thought I saw a woman standing just inside the door with a pair of binoculars."

"In case they are looking for us, Sergey stretch out like you're sleeping, and I'm going to put this seat back, so it looks like there's only one person in this car. Head for the highway and don't speed." Andrei cautioned.

They continued on the highway to Montréal and were happy to see the plane head in that direction. They had three and a half hours to go when the plane they were watching landed at the Pierre Trudeau Airport. Andrei spoke with the agents on the ground to make sure the Americans were followed. Knowing that the plane was landing at the private jet hangar made them easier to track, and the agent soon followed them to a house in a residential neighborhood near Summit Woods. At least they had the new location of the Americans, and it should be relatively easy to attack them there.

"Perhaps we should think of another way to get rid of them? After our previous two attempts with the guns which brought law enforcement down on us, maybe we should revert to poison. It leaves less of a trail," Sergey suggested.

"Let's discuss our options on the drive," Andrei said.

CHAPTER 18

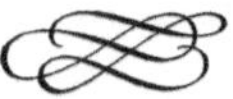

Jill and her friends loved the rare convenience of riding on a private plane. It was more comfortable, and eliminated the hassle of security and baggage collection. Henrik had another stretch limo waiting for them for their journey to the house. The travel had been so smooth and uneventful, it was like they were visiting a friend's house that was an hour away.

Henrik's security staff had done more than add security for them, as someone had also stocked the refrigerator and the wine cooler. They were able to quickly drop their baggage and meet in the dining room to plan the next few days in the Province of Québec. It was still afternoon, and Henrik had a favorite restaurant he wanted them to try but suggested they visit the Basilica of Notre-Dame, which was two blocks from the restaurant. It was a spectacular church and on everyone's list of places to see.

"That sounds like a good plan. I would love to give thanks to our Lord for our survival yesterday and today. After all the excitement and travel, we can relax in a nice restaurant, then I'll have an early evening and head home. You young people can stay out and do the town as they say," Hope said.

"I'm with you, Hope," Jill replied. "I've been up since four this morning, and the two adrenaline rushes in twenty-four hours has really zapped me. I apologize in advance if I fall asleep in the amazing church or at dinner."

Jack and Marie echoed Jill's thoughts. Angela looked at Nathan and said, "Maybe you, Jo, and I can stay awake and plan our next couple of days here. I want to go to Québec City at some point, and I know it's like a two and a half-hour drive, so that will take all of one of our days."

Nathan was nervous about the security of the house and asked, "Henrik, tell me what security you've installed here. It feels like this house would be easy to break into. These Russians are unrelenting and creative. I have to think by now they've figured out Jill's connection to the other Russian citizens that she's helped send to prison."

"Sure, you've been to my home in Stuttgart, so you know what I'm capable of. Let me talk about this house. As you saw, when we pulled up, there's a gated entrance and a stone wall surrounding the house. The stone wall is electrified. If someone tries to get into the yard by swinging in any of the trees, hidden under the leaves are spring nets that will entangle them. I added bolts and locks to the gate. I also tried a new technology. I've put a film on all the windows that blacks out the window from the outside, but gives you a polarized view inside the house. That way, none of us can be spotted in a window for a sniper. We also have cameras everywhere for motion and recording with my German staff monitoring it."

"The Russians like to poison their enemies. So what can we do about that?" Marie asked, looking up from a search on her phone.

"I've spent some time thinking about that, and I think I have the house protected. What we need to worry about is our hands touching a contaminated surface and food. I think they prefer car doors and front doors. I think our best bet there is simply to wear gloves when we're out in public. Fortunately, it's fall, and we won't look out of place with gloves on."

"Couldn't the poison soak through our gloves?" Jo asked. Her anxiety was climbing higher and higher as the conversation continued. These Russians were scary dudes.

"I had my team drop off gloves for our use. They're all black, there's a box of a hundred for each person, and we have thin glove liners, so your hands don't sweat. They're neoprene and should protect us from most acids and agents used for pesticides. They won't protect us from radioactive agents, and there's nothing we can do about that other than walking around in a lead suit."

"And food?" Jill asked.

"I think our Russian friends will arrive in Montréal after we're seated at the restaurant, but after tonight, I think we'll have to enjoy Nathan and Mrs. Weber's cooking. There are recent cases where ricin has been put in tea and other agents in liquids. Liquids are a bigger problem than food, and I think we're safe buying food from anywhere that we can see the kitchen and watch the food prep."

"You've given this a lot more thought than I had. Thank you," Jill said, reaching out to hug Henrik.

Henrik was surprised by the simple words and the hug.

"Security is my business. As the world has become more complicated, I've had to move beyond cameras and computer programs. When we sign on a new client, we start with a threat assessment. Who are the client's enemies, and what are the risks? Is the client a company based entirely on the brilliance of a CEO that will collapse if the CEO is killed? Is there a risk of theft of intellectual property? Is the client operating in a non-secure environment like Afghanistan? Is there travel and family to protect also? I was awake at four in the morning today because I was doing our own threat assessment, which included significant research on what the Russians are up to as they seem to be our only enemies at the moment. I put my company to work finding a location that we could shore up with added protection, and then I looked at our risks when we're away from this home. After all, we all want to see Montréal and Québec City as we're here on vacation," Henrik said with a small smile.

"That's an elaborate answer to a simple question," Nathan said. "I agreed with Jill when she told the Canadian authorities that going home to California wouldn't solve this problem. I'm glad we have you to protect us from the Russians, as you seem to be the most capable person on the planet to do so. I love cooking, and with Hope's assistance, we'll keep everyone well fed. Unfortunately, we won't be able to sample the French cuisine of this region."

"Yes, but it's better to live another day, then eat tainted food," Jill said.

"I don't mind saying this, you guys have me scared to leave this house," Jack said.

"This is the supreme test of my company. Can I protect my best friends from a multiplicity of weapons used by the Russians? I've taken this very seriously, and we'll actually have a security detail when we're out and about. Angela, we'll get to Québec City, but we'll do so on my plane. That will reduce our vulnerability on the highway. I also have some of my best computer hackers targeting Russia at the moment. We need some leverage to get them permanently off our collective backs. Even as I think I can keep you safe here in Canada, we're all going to leave and go home to our respective cities. There is an unlimited number of Russian agents that can be sent after us, so we need a permanent solution. I just don't know what it is yet," Henrik said.

There was silence in the house as they all processed his words. He had given more thought to their problems than the rest of them combined, and for that, they were deeply grateful.

"Personally, the best words I heard was that you were looking for a permanent solution to get the Russians off our back. I'm not a computer hack, but I can find all kinds of sneaky information about people and organizations. How can I help your company's staff find leverage?" Marie asked.

Henrik smiled and enveloped Marie in a hug, "That is why you're my friends! When faced with an army of Russian assassins, you don't wilt and fall apart. Instead, you take up arms and shoot."

"Is that a famous German proverb?" Jo asked. "Sort of your version of, 'keep a stiff upper lip'."

"I think I learned that from your American football. I think your expression is 'when the going gets tough, the tough get going'.

"That will do, and speaking of getting going, the Basilica closes in just over an hour. Let's go!" Angela said.

In no time, they piled into two non-specific silver sedans waiting with drivers in the garage.

"These are my people, and I thought I'd make it more difficult for the Russians to follow us. It's nice that we all fit into a stretch limousine, but if we do that, we may as well post our destinations on a highway billboard," Henrik said.

Everyone nodded and piled into the cars. By the time they reached the Basilica, Angela knew all the details about their drivers. They were German citizens who spoke French and English in addition to their native German. They had completed the evasive driving class offered by BMW.

"Are you armed with any weapons?" Nathan asked their driver.

"No, sir. It is not legal to carry any weapons, including guns, knives, and pepper spray in Canada. However, I understand from Mr. Klein that you have a Master Black Belt in Hapkido. I'm a Master Black Belt in Krav Maga. I trained in Israel. The other driver is similarly trained."

"Excellent. I can relax," Nathan said, settling into the seat.

Jill had worked her way up to a blue belt in Tai Chi, but she would never have the power and strength in her moves that Nathan did. Still, she could outrun him, but neither of them was faster than a speeding bullet. It was a grim thought, but Henrik was right that they needed to work to think beyond snipers. When they returned from dinner, she was going to do some serious research on Russian poisons if she could stay awake. From what she remembered about past murders, none of them occurred in large crowds. Jill guessed that was because it was harder to be secretive and not get caught on cameras when there were many witnesses to an event.

"Are we being followed at the moment?" Jill asked of the driver.

"We are. We'll be doing some evasive driving once we clear this residential area and hit the highway. There's only one car, so this will be easy. The car in front of us will make a clean getaway, and then we will quickly follow."

Jill thought she might enjoy watching this, and she'd try and take some mental notes for the next time that someone went after them. She remembered when Nick and she were being chased down Boreas Pass road, and an SUV wanted to push them off the edge. He'd help her hold it together until they ended up in a prairie, and not driving off a steep cliff.

Henrik was seated on one side of her, and Marie was on the other. Marie asked, "Are you thinking of that time you had a car try and push you off the road in Colorado?"

"Yeah, Nick came to my rescue because he'd taken an evasive driving course. I'm sure we're in good hands with your drivers. Do you think this is our Mr. Tamm behind us?"

"No. They would have had to drive to Montréal as I doubt they can get through any airport security at this point. I think they are probably still an hour out from this city. So hopefully, that's not a sniper in the car behind us. Though, it's not like Russia has only one of them."

Their driver said something into a headset, Jill presumed, to the car in front of them. They would need to coordinate their actions; otherwise, the tail would simply attach itself to the other car. She saw the highway ahead. She was tempted to look out the back window, but what would that achieve? There was nothing she could do to add to her group's protection that Henrik hadn't already thought of.

"Maybe they're after you, Henrik, since you're a famous CEO of a company that has the technology to detect the Russians," Nathan suggested.

"I don't think so. Your partner has taken down how many Russians behaving badly?"

"No more than three or four," Jill said. "But I did them a favor getting rid of their serial killer/hit girl. She was crazy and likely uncontrollable by the Russians."

They watched their driver follow the other car up onto the freeway and accelerate. Then three exits later, their lead car made a dive for the off-ramp and was gone.

"Did anyone follow them?" Marie asked.

"No, I just saw the driver make a call on his cell, so he's notifying someone that the two cars split up. Oh, and this is interesting. He's decided to ride our tail, so he doesn't lose us. He probably thinks we are aware of the tail, and he's right."

Now Jill couldn't resist looking back, and like their car, she saw a silver sedan that looked like a hundred other cars.

"What are you going to do?"

"I'm going to make a series of lane changes over the next one to four exits, and I'll catch them off guard at some point, and exit before they can do so." Jill heard the odd horn honked at them, but she didn't care. The other drivers around them had no clue that they were being chased by a Russian assassin. Better to irk the natives, then let the Russians win.

On the third freeway exit, their driver managed to break free of the surveillance car with the help of a couple semi-trucks, and a curve in the road.

"Did you know about that curve in advance?" Nathan asked.

"Yes," the driver said, smiling, amused about the interest of the Americans.

"You know that we three Americans are backseat drivers, and we'll give you driving advice whether you need it or not."

"Yes, Mr. Klein warned me that I might have driving help from my passengers," the driver grinned.

"Henrik knows all of our behaviors by now," Marie said, smiling at the man they were all talking about.

The driver continued to occasionally watch his mirrors, but there was no other activity.

"All is clear, and the Basilica is coming up on our right. Call me when you need me."

They bailed out of the car and looked around for Jo, Jack, Angela, and Hope. The Basilica took up a full block, and their friends had been dropped off on another street with instructions on how to join up with the others.

They went inside the beautiful old church to gaze at the stained glass windows, statues, and beautiful wood and tile decorating the altar. Hope and Angela spent time in quiet reflection and prayer in one of the pews while the remainder walked around, looking at the small chapels lining the church.

Jill recognized the pipes of an organ and groaned silently. She'd never again feel completely safe in a church near the organ pipes after watching the piano player die by ice arrow. She felt a hand come over her shoulder and jumped since she was lost in her own thoughts.

"Sorry didn't mean to scare you," Nathan whispered as no one had a loud voice in church.

They heard bells announce that the church would be closing for Mass, and worshipers were welcome to stay, but for everyone else, the church was closed for the day. At least that's what Jill thought they said as the announcement came in French.

"Let's walk to the restaurant as soon as Angela and Hope are ready to leave the church. There's no reason to rush them."

As a group, they meandered toward the exit and pretty much managed to assemble all at the same time.

"Ready?" Nathan asked the group, and with nods, they followed Henrik and Marie's lead toward the restaurant. Jill was too tired to keep an eye out for evil Russians. She walked along with her hand in Nathan's while he watched out for suspicious characters. He knew that Henrik had men in the area as well. Still, he was getting used to these precarious situations with Jill. They'd been dating going on three years, and he'd been on more adventures in those years than for the entirety of the rest of his life.

They arrived at a charming French restaurant and followed the hostess into a private room. The wine was excellent, though Jill had hers with a cup of coffee. Not exactly the right wine pairing, but she needed something to boost her flagging energy.

Jill looked around the room after they were served their beverage of choice and felt the need to hold her glass up, stopping all of the individual conversations among her friends.

"I want to say thank you all for continuing to be my friends. I've endangered each and every one of you several times on this trip alone, but still, you're here, and you're smiling. Love you, and that's the end of my sappy speech."

She was met with applause, and many 'love you back,' replies from everyone in the room. Sometimes a sappy statement was all she had to offer to the most amazing set of friends a woman could have.

They were just finishing their meals when Jill received a call from a Montréal area code. She decided to answer it as she hadn't received many spam calls while in Canada. She wasn't sure if that was due to her iPhone software changes, or if the Canadian telecom companies were better at blocking spam.

"Hello,"

"Hello, is this Dr. Jill Quint?" came a voice in English that was lightly accented.

"Yes. Who's calling?"

"I'm Lieutenant Simonetta Martel of the Major Crimes Unit of the Montréal Police. I would like to meet with you tonight. When is a convenient time?"

Jill looked at her watch and calculated when they would arrive home from the restaurant.

"How about an hour from now? Do you have a pen and paper to write down my address?"

"Detective-Sargent Hassan passed it on to me unless you've changed your address."

"No, Lieutenant, we haven't. We have high security at the house we're staying at, and so please ring again when you arrive so that I may open the gates. We don't want to leave them open, waiting for your arrival."

"Oui, I shall see you soon."

Jill closed her phone and looked at her friends who'd ended their own conversations to listen to what she was saying.

"A Montréal Police Detective is going to meet with us in an hour. She'll call me when she arrives as I don't want the gates opened unnecessarily. It will disrupt the wonderful security system that Henrik has in place."

"So much for you going to bed early," Nathan said.

"I rather the police be our partners from the start, then have to explain ourselves when our lives are in peril. Since the Lieutenant called my cell phone, she must have been briefed by her colleagues in Toronto. I hope that gives us legitimacy as it seems we have to re-establish it with each law enforcement agency, and that gets old fast."

CHAPTER 19

On their way north towards Montréal, Andrei had been keeping in touch with his fellow agents in that city. He was starting to feel embarrassed that he couldn't manage to kill a woman and her three friends. Her group was a large target. They weren't trained in special ops as far as he could tell from everything they'd read online and a Russian intelligence report. Why was she so damn hard to kill? If he didn't complete this mission fast, his reputation would be getting him a ticket to Siberia. Once he crossed over from Alaska to Russia, he would be stationed there for years to come, the FSB would see to that. If he stayed in North America, he would constantly be looking over his shoulder while on the run.

He needed to kill them tonight, complete the assignment, and move on to new challenges. He usually liked to observe his target for some time, before pulling the trigger and killing them. That way, he had time to discover their habits and a location that wouldn't set a trap for him, but he was feeling desperate, and there was the allure of a residence. How easy was that going to be to target them? There would be no lobby staff to get by or cameras on every floor. It was evening by the time they arrived in

Montréal. They checked into a hotel, changed clothing, ate, checked their rifles and semi-automatic weapons to make sure they were ready, and studied Google Earth around their target house.

Andrei said to Alexey and Sergey, "I think the three of us should be able to cover the house. I don't know anything about our agents in Montréal. I don't know if they're strictly intelligence, or if they have any arms training. We could end up accidentally killing these agents if they don't know what they're doing. Do you agree?"

"There are eight of them. Can we keep them contained in the house? There are probably more than two doors, given the size of that house," Sergey said.

"If we blocked the door to the street, and they escape into the backyard, I bet none of them can scale that wall, so we can shoot them there," Alexey said.

"Yes. It's doubtful that they will all be in one room. I think we'll wind up chasing some of them through the house or into the backyard. That gives them time to call the cops. So I would suggest that we be out of there within three minutes, two if we can do it," Andrei said.

His men nodded, and he searched for pictures of the interior of the house. If it sold in the last decade, there were likely pictures on some real estate websites, including those of the backyard. He found what he was looking for, and the men studied the house's interior and backyard.

"They could escape through the garage and out the front. I don't see a place one of us can stand, and cover both doors," Sergey said.

"I think you're right, Sergey. I'm going to call for one of our agents to join us. No matter their training, all we need them to do is stand with their back to the door, with a rifle across their chest. We don't even have to put bullets in the gun, they'll be there strictly as a threat," Andrei said.

Andrei went through the complicated process of contacting the agents in Montréal with the message that one of them should meet them at their hotel. An agent would be there soon was the response he received. He took a break and stretched. It had been a long day starting with the chase on the lake that morning. Being cooped up in a car for five hours between Montréal and Toronto drove him nuts. Now he felt a glimmer of excitement that came before any well-executed operation. He just needed one additional man to complete this effort.

There was a knock on the hotel door, and after verification, an agent named Valery Pechyonkin was introduced to Andrei's team. He did not look thrilled when told the details of the operation. He lived a quiet and peaceful life attached to the Consulate in Montréal. He was content to listen in on conversations where directed by Mother Russia. He had arms training but hadn't carried a gun since arriving in Canada three years ago. The idea of holding a Kalashnikov across his chest scared him. He relaxed slightly when Andrei said it would be unloaded. The tough-looking Russian apparently sensed his discomfort with guns.

"I think we should plan to carry out this mission around eight-thirty tonight. At that hour, they should be home and drinking wine in the living room of the house. If we go earlier, they may have not returned yet, and if we go later, we could end up chasing them through all the bedrooms of the house, which would take time."

Andrei received notification from the agent watching the street near the target house that the Americans had returned. It seemed that it had also been a long day for them, as this was seen as early to be returning home. A short time later, they received a second call, that a female had arrived with a passenger, and been admitted through the front gates of the home.

"Should we wait till she leaves?" Valery asked, looking for any reason to delay his involvement with this murderous scheme.

Andrei considered and replied. "No. If they have a visitor,

they're more likely to be gathered in one room and relaxed. It's a good time to corner and kill them. When you're using an automatic weapon, it's not difficult for the gun spray to kill an additional person or two."

Valery tried to think of any reason to get out of the clutches of this murderous trio, but he knew if he ran, he'd be their first murder of the night. If this is what he had to do to keep this wonderful post in Montréal, he'd suck it up and do it. After all, he didn't have to actually shoot anyone; he only had to carry the gun and block an exit, while they terrorized and killed people.

Andrei outfitted them with balaclavas, gloves, and a change of clothing for Valery, who'd arrived in blue jeans. Before they left the hotel, they discussed taking one car or two. They agreed on two as that gave them more opportunities for a safe escape. They would park on the street the house was located on and put another car on the street behind. It would mean climbing over some walls, but they were carrying a rope with them in a backpack, and it was all about getting away safely.

They reviewed their plans one more time, synchronized burner phones, and then tossed back a shot of vodka with a toast to good health. Thirty minutes later, they were on a winding, hilly street, lined with expensive cars parked in front of extraordinary homes. The second car was in a similar neighborhood looking for a dark area to park. They moved quietly and efficiently to get in place. Two at the front gate, one at each side wall. Andrei gave the countdown for them to scale their fences.

"Ouch!" muttered Valery, and he heard expletives in Russian across the phones.

He'd placed his hands on the top of the wall to climb it and had been painfully shocked. He wasn't going to try that again. He stood in the dark, waiting for instructions. He listened as Andrei and Sergey discussed what had caused the shock. Then they saw bright spotlights turned on, and suddenly it looked like daylight around the home.

Andrei made the call, "Abort this mission, back to the cars, now!"

They all scampered back over the walls, and down the road to their respective cars. They heard sirens in the distance as they drove out of the neighborhood at the posted speed limit, and away from the sirens. They arrived back at the hotel, glad to have escaped detection.

"Why didn't the agents watching the house notice the additional security? I'm sure that was put in for the Americans," Andrei raged, holding his hands up to show the burns from the live wires. He'd taken his gloves off to operate his phone while the others still had their gloves on when they touched the wires. He grabbed his rifle and aimed it at the wall. Then he put it down and pulled the ammunition out of it. He then pointed it again and pressed the trigger. It made his hand hurt, but he didn't think it would affect his aim.

Valery replied, "I followed them from the airport, and I didn't see anyone near the fences when I tailed them to that location. Then I followed them from the residence, but I lost them along the way. Maybe while we were gone, they had work done, or before they arrived."

"Valery, you are such an idiot. How could you lose them when you followed them from their home?"

"They knew I was back there and took evasive action to avoid me. I wasn't trained on tailing people in cars before I left Russia," came his fearful reply. He wasn't sure he was going to still be alive at the end of this night.

"Okay, Comrade, enough. What do we do now?" asked Sergey. He could tell the Montréal station agent was going to be worthless for the most part. He was a warm body on their side and nothing more. He had no special skills to help with this operation.

Andrei still had adrenaline running through him from their plan falling to pieces. His hands hurt, and he hadn't had enough sleep in the past three days. He felt like punching the wall, but his hands were in too much pain to do that. Now he wanted to kill this Jill Quint as much as Mother Russia wanted her dead, but first, he had to think.

"There's nothing more we can do tonight. I want an agent on the house so we can see if they go anywhere. I'd like to get someone walking a dog in that area, so we don't look like we're loitering in the neighborhood. I'd like to throw some GPS or listening devices if we can catch up to any of their cars or people. So let's load up our people with those items. Do you understand, Valery?"

"Yes sir," he replied, knowing the implied threat was he would be dead if he didn't get these instructions right. It all felt very unfair as the operation falling apart had nothing to do with him directly. He'd make sure Andrei's orders were followed out, then find another agent to pawn these three brutes on. If he had to get a violent case of food poisoning, that was a far better scenario than spending any additional time in their company.

CHAPTER 20

The group returned from dinner and settled into the living room, planning the remainder of their trip, or in Henrik's case, checking in with his company to see what they found on the Russians. Jill leaned back against the sofa cushion and stared at the ceiling, thinking about the facts of this case, but nothing was coming to her. Hope excused herself to call it an early night. She had no need to meet this latest cop that was stopping by.

Jill was startled when her phone rang as she had been on the verge of drifting off to sleep. The detective was at her gate.

A short time later, the detective was inside, accompanied by Officer Simpson from the CIA.

"You just can't keep away from our exciting company, can you?" Jill said.

"Just trying to coordinate with our Canadian friends. Why did you choose a house instead of a hotel? I would have thought you'd be better protected in a large hotel."

"Henrik made some modifications to this home that makes it more secure than hotel security. You forget he runs a major German company that knows how to protect its CEO. We're just the lucky recipients of that attention and expertise. So what kind of update do you have for us? We toured the Basilica and had dinner in the neighborhood of the church, but we were followed there until our driver took evasive action and lost the car on the highway. That tells us the Russians know we're in Montréal. Furthermore, they know where we're staying," Jill said.

"I'm not surprised. There's a Russian Consulate General here in Montréal, and so I think they probably picked your trail up at the airport while the other group drove north. I don't think they can get through airport security at the moment. Also, we've done additional research on some of the parties involved with this case," said Officer Simpson.

"And what did you learn?"

"They're operating a cell here that was meant to support the piano player. However, they likely lacked faith in him from the start. We think Nikita Chernov might have had a complete mental breakdown while in Russia. During his recovery, he met Anna and members of the FSB. Whether he was aware of their connections is unknown, nor is it known what Nikita really thought of Anna. We don't know if he was bamboozled, or if this was an arranged marriage as part of the cover."

"What did you learn from her since she's been in your custody?" Jill asked.

"We have learned that she's a supremely good actress," Simpson replied with a look of pain on his face.

Jill raised an eyebrow at his response.

"Her defection from her Russian handlers was a charade. It took us some time to catch on."

Detective Martel hadn't heard this part of the story and so asked, "How were you alerted to her scheme?"

"Actually, we were never suspicious. She disappeared from the safe house, and at first, we thought the Russians had located and kidnapped her. Then as part of our normal schedule for a safe house, we brought in a detector for radio-frequency, and the alarm bells went off. She dropped what our experts are calling a third-generation listening device everywhere she visited."

"Did Russia hear any state secrets?" Jill asked.

"No, as none were discussed in any of these locations. They did learn how America handles defectors and how we keep them protected, but that changes with each protectee."

"So she disappeared into the United States, and no one knows where she is. As a Russian agent of some sort, she should be quite capable of staying hidden."

"We do know where she's hiding, and it's not in the U.S. Which is where our Canadian colleagues come in."

"Did you know about her disappearance this morning when we met for the first time?" Jill asked.

Now he really looked chagrined, and he said, "Yes."

"So why were you hiding this information from me as someone was trying to kill us this morning?"

Detective Martel's head had been bouncing like a ping-pong between Simpson and Jill. Before she had the chance to insert questions, the American woman would ask them for her.

"Look, we routinely keep information close to our chest, so to speak, and you're no different. This is classified information on a need to know basis."

Jill was too tired to fight Simpson over the risks he was taking by not dialing in Jill and her friends, the apparent target of a Russian special team. She was about to tell him to get out of the house, and then have a civil conversation with the Detective, after all, they were on her territory when alarms began to sound.

"What's the alarm for?" Jill asked Henrik, leaving the couch to go over and chat with him, where he was seated at the dining room table.

"We've just had four men try to scale our fences. They've been shocked by the wires on top of the fences, and bright lights are about to come on as though it were daylight."

"This I got to see," said the detective walking over to the

window to peer out at her car. "Very impressive, I'm not sure the Montréal Police could do any better at protecting this house."

She called in the need for backup to her dispatcher, knowing the men would be long gone by the time any squad cars got there.

Jill leaned over Henrik's shoulder to look at his laptop screen, which had the perimeter cameras on it. Not only was their property covered by cameras, but they were also infrared cameras. That was how Henrik had been able to count four men. He turned the bright lights off once they got out of the range of the cameras.

The detective said, "The lights are out, and I can't see anything out there."

"Yes, the men are gone from this property, and so there is nothing to see. I don't want your department to have to field more questions than necessary about the bright lights. This is overall a quiet neighborhood," Henrik said, and then he grimaced when he heard the sirens in the distance.

The detective made another call, and they heard the sirens quiet as she said, "There's no reason to announce their arrival to the Russians, assuming that's who just tried to scale your walls. Perhaps, Mr. Klein, you could briefly turn on the lights once my men arrive so we can look for anything they might have dropped after they got that electrical shock from the top of your wall.

He nodded. There hadn't been much noise inside the home as Henrik muted the alarms. Angela had walked over to the hallway leading to her mother's bedroom. She leaned into the bedroom and would've said something if her mother was awake, but she heard soft snores. She closed the door and returned to the living room and her little group that was planning the remainder of their vacation. There was no imminent threat from the intruders, and she could not assist the Montréal Police, so it was time to go back to what she could do, which was vacation planning.

The detective observed the other members of this group resuming whatever they had been doing when she arrived. They were a remarkably calm group with not a one worried that their lives were in danger. They must know this Mr. Klein so well that they had complete faith in his ability to keep them safe. Fascinating. She wondered what other stuff was outside protecting the house and its occupants that she didn't know about. Guns, knives, and pepper spray, which were commonplace protective weapons in the United States, were nowhere to be seen in this group. There was probably a building code that made electrifying the walls illegal, but she wasn't going to worry about it. It had flashed across her brain when the alarm initially sounded that she was one detective, not even carrying a weapon, whose duty it would've been to defend the eight occupants of this house against unknown Russian resources. She'd gotten a report from the event that morning and knew those resources likely included a sniper with the gun. She was grateful she would eventually go home to her family that night, not having to defend against any Russian weapons.

The detective went outside to meet her responding officers, and they did a search of the property, but the only thing they found was a new piece of rope near one of the side walls. One of the men must have dropped it, they bagged it for evidence, but as three of the four men were wearing gloves in the video recording of the attack, it was unlikely to yield any information.

Once the commotion died down, Jill turned to Officer Simpson and said, "Let's finish the story here. I was about to throw you out of this house as it's clear that the safety of my team and I are not important to you or your agency, but frankly, I'm too tired to muster the energy. Do you know where Anna Chernov is at this moment?"

She could see a range of emotions cross the face of Officer Simpson as he debated whether to tell her another untruth, "Yes. She's inside the Russian Embassy in Ottawa."

Jill had watched his face as he made the statement, and near as she could tell, it was the truth.

Detective Martel asked the question that was on the tip of Jill's tongue, "How do you know that?"

"We have a history with Russia going back a millennium. Rule number one is to never trust them. Even though this female seemed to have truly defected, we needed to assume first and foremost that she was an agent of some Russian agency. Her emotions about her husband seemed muted rather than passionate. We watched her behavior for several days while she was in our custody, and we never got comfortable with her. We planted tiny GPS devices in her lipstick case and in a tube of mascara as those were the items she arrived with and frequently used. Once we knew she was missing, we activated the trackers."

"How did she cross the Canadian Border? Did you put a bulletin out on her?" Martel asked.

"We didn't start tracking her immediately as she left in the middle of the night. By the time we turned the tracker on, she was already in Buffalo, NY."

"Buffalo? Why would she go there?" Marie asked, curious about the Russian woman that she was the first to identify as part of this investigation.

Simpson paused another moment and said, "It seems that you were correct to focus on the Toronto Conductor."

"Who is this Conductor? I don't remember my colleagues in Toronto saying anything about a conductor," Martel asked.

"Dr. Quint here thought it was unusual that a Russian Conductor from the Toronto Philharmonic Orchestra would be close to her friends when they were tourists at Niagara Falls. Turns out, she was right. Your colleagues were afraid to target the Russian community, given that it is so large in Toronto. Who would have thought an Orchestra Conductor would have anything to do with a Russian spy network?"

"I'm with my Toronto colleagues. Niagara Falls is a top tourist destination. Why wouldn't you find Russian-Canadians visiting?"

"The conductor ended up being in two photographs taken near

the Falls. It was too big of a coincidence that the man would end up being at both sites. There was no other person in the background of the two photos. Furthermore, the conductor was in the audience for the piano recital. Somehow I don't think that's how he finds piano players for his orchestra."

"Maybe he just wanted to go to a live music event as a spectator?" said the Lieutenant.

"That could've been true, but as he was the only Russian that popped up in multiple locations, I felt further research was warranted. Your Toronto colleagues disagreed with me. So Officer Simpson, what role did the orchestra conductor have in Anna Chernov's escape into Canada?" Jill asked.

"She crossed into Canada with the orchestra on their bus. She was listed as a violin player. From Toronto, someone gave her a ride to the Russian Embassy in Ottawa, and then they must have scanned her as the tracker went dead. She's out of our reach now."

"What if she killed the piano player, her husband?" Martel asked.

"She couldn't have. She was in our custody at the time of his murder."

"So, what's your plan?" Jill asked, looking at her visitors. "Clearly, the Russians aren't going to leave my team alone. Don't bother telling me to go home as the Russians will follow me. This is going to be resolved while we're in Canada. Besides, the Toronto police still don't have a suspect for Nikita Chernov's murder."

Jill looked at Lieutenant Martel and Officer Simpson and knew she had put them on the spot. She was tired and cranky and knew she wasn't an equal partner in the effort to contain the Russians and figure out which one of them killed the piano player. She was also confident with whatever protections Henrik had put in and around the house, she was well protected when she was home. She would take a look in the morning to see what everyone wanted to sightsee.

"Look, I'm exhausted. I think we're done here, and I'll call you the next time the Russians are taking potshots at my team. The two of you do not have a plan at the moment to deal with this situation. You're wasting my time and energy. Let me show you to the door, and you can email me when you have a plan."

Jill stood up and walked over to her front door and stood there waiting for Martel and Simpson to exit. She could've heard a pin drop in the silence in the house. The two guests stood up and exited without another word. She closed her eyes and leaned against the front door for a moment of peace. Then she straightened and looked around intent on saying her goodnights to everyone and finding her bed.

"What?"

"They disappointed you again," Nathan said.

"Yeah, they did, and my brain cells have hit a wall. I can't think about anything other than going to sleep. See you all in the morning," Jill said around a yawn.

She heard various "goodnights" called out by everyone as she climbed the stairs to their bedroom. She was asleep almost the moment she put her head down on the pillow.

CHAPTER 21

Jill was the first one up the next morning. After getting a cup of coffee, she glanced over at what was planned for the day. It seemed that they would be visiting an art museum, a Ferris wheel of sorts, and a walking tour of the Old Montréal. It sounded like a fun day, and she felt confident that Henrik's people could defend them. She then went over to the dining room table where she'd left her case notes from the night before. It was time to take another look at them, just to see if she missed anything. There was also an email from Detective Ireland from the previous night forwarding new results of the autopsy. The new item was Nikita had cocobolo sawdust on his clothing. The lab thought that the sawdust came from the melted ice arrow as the sawdust would make the ice stronger. Jill had a degree in botany, but she couldn't recall ever hearing about wood made from a cocobolo tree. She did a search, and it was a rare tree in Central America. It was extremely hard, expensive, and rare, and it was used to make musical instruments, chess pieces, and pool cues. Better still, there were few places you could buy it, and it stained the hands of anyone with prolonged exposure to the wood. Wouldn't that be great evidence at trial if they could find an archer with red-stained hands?

She went back through all the pictures and video stills they had collected at anytime during the case to see if she noticed anyone with red-stained hands. Then she saw it. The man that was partially identified as Sergey Shishin had a red hand resting outside of his car's open window when he was staking out their hotel in Canada.

She looked at the time, and it was just coming on six in the morning – too early to call the detective. So she sent him the image in question and a botany journal description of the wood. He was the archer or an accessory to the archer as he had shaved the cocobolo tree for its sawdust, and his hands had absorbed the red-staining oil. That sawdust had then been used in the ice that formed the arrow to add strength to the arrow. She sent off the email and returned to the evidence. They likely had the man on two counts of attempted murder as she'd bet he was one of the shooters in the boat yesterday. The CIA had a man on the look-out, and Jill wondered if he'd taken any pictures of the approaching boat. They were so secretive about everything that he wouldn't have volunteered that information, but perhaps it was collected by them.

She sent a second email to Officer Simpson with the question as to whether any pictures had been taken of the boat that chased them. Maybe she could find Mr. Red Hands on board, and they would have another charge of attempted murder.

Jill then paused a moment in the early dawn to ask herself what she was doing? Why was she wasting any vacation time on this case when the law enforcement types had proven to be incon-siderate of her team's welfare and of her as a partner? She looked up when she saw Mom heading for the kitchen in her bathrobe. Jill was sitting in the dark and didn't want to scare her.

"Hey, Mom," she called out in a cheery voice.

She saw her put her hand over her heart, and so Jill added, "I was sitting in the dark thinking, and I didn't want to scare you."

"Better that you called out before I had a hot cup of coffee in my hand. What are you thinking about in the dark?"

"Some new information came back from the autopsy, and I sent off a few emails to Detective Ireland and Officer Simpson with different questions. Then I asked myself why I was doing that? I should be enjoying my time with you and my friends."

She finished getting a cup of coffee and came over to sit down in the living room, turning on a light in the area.

"I think you're doing it for a couple of reasons, and those reasons are the core of you and why your friends love you."

"Are you sure? I'm worried that my ego is driving this – I have a need to prove something to law enforcement types."

"I think there's a little of that in your passion for this case, but I think it's more likely that they have been slow to recognize the danger of these lads, and so most of your desire is more about protecting us. I also think there's a small affinity from all of us who watched the man play beautiful music one moment and then keel over backward in the next."

"So, what should I do differently?" Jill asked.

"I don't think you should do anything differently. Your friends aren't upset with your behavior. The only ones that have created conflict are the very people who should be better at finding this murderer than you are."

"To be fair to them, they have to follow rules that we don't."

"Okay, why don't you spend the day being a tourist with us. Henrik seems to have good protection for us, and while that doesn't catch these hoodlums, it does keep us safe. Maybe taking a break from all of this will clear your head, and you can find the solution tonight or tomorrow."

Jill reached over and closed her laptop and said, "Great idea. I'll take your advice. Thanks, Mom."

"What would you like for breakfast?"

"You don't have to make me anything. You're here on vacation, not to cook for me."

"I enjoy cooking. I'm awake, so I may as well be useful and start thinking about breakfast. Nathan won't be up for hours if I recall, so maybe I'll make a frittata or quiche for everyone. We can all start out with a good breakfast."

"Okay, then let me help if you need stuff cut, or whipped, or shredded, and I'll be your sous chef."

They worked together in companionable silence creating a large pan of the egg concoction. Marie entered the kitchen, followed by Henrik.

"There are good scents wafting up the stairs. What are you cooking?" Henrik asked Hope.

"It's an Italian dish – a frittata. It's full of eggs and cheese, ham, onions, green peppers. Is that something you would eat for breakfast?"

"You bet, it sounds and smells delicious. What's our schedule today?"

"We're visiting a museum, a park, and doing a walking tour of Old Montréal," Jill said.

"Excellent, I'll enjoy walking about. Yesterday involved too much sitting," Marie said. "Are you doing any work on the case?"

"Mom and I were just talking about that. I sent some new information to Detective Ireland and Officer Simpson because it came in overnight, and I have no plan to do any more work on this case. We just need to watch our backs, and I'm sure Henrik has a plan of how we can stay safe."

"Now that I know our plans, I'll get together with my team and plan our security. Did anyone check the weather today?"

"I just did," Marie said, holding her phone. "Of course, it's in Fahrenheit rather than Celsius, but it's supposed to be clear till tonight, and then an overnight shower, and clear again tomorrow for when we head to Québec City."

"That's good news. I'm not sure I would've enjoyed a walking tour of Old Montréal in the rain," Hope said. "This will be ready in about twenty minutes. I'm going to change into better clothes, and I'll be back in time to serve breakfast."

There was a chorus of, "Take all the time you need, Mom. We can serve ourselves."

She smiled and left the kitchen, but they could read in her eyes that she would be back in time to serve breakfast.

"What time are we leaving?" asked Henrik.

"The museum doesn't open until ten, and I think we should do that first. That way, when we walk outdoors in the park and through old Montréal, it will be warmer. That also gives our late risers more time to sleep," Marie suggested.

"Normally, I would wake up our late risers to get going on our day, but it's been a stressful couple of days, and everyone deserves their sleep. Maybe I'll read up on the history of Montréal and Québec City, so I can enjoy these tours with more understanding of where the cities have come from," Jill said.

"I'll go inform our security detail what we are doing today so they can plan."

"Please give them my thanks. Without them, we wouldn't be able to enjoy our time here," Jill said.

"Actually, my company is thinking about expanding into personal protective services, and when we ran into trouble in Toronto, I had their team leader and his crew fly here. There's a guest house out back that they're staying in. Going up against the Russians is a tough assignment, but it is what we would expect if we were protecting people in some of the volatile parts of the world."

"Wow, that's pressure when your first assignment is to keep your CEO and his friends alive," Marie said.

"Yes, but it's also a heck of a way to prove that you are the right person for the job," Henrik said as he left to walk over to the guest house in the backyard.

"We are so lucky to have him as a friend," Jill said. "I wish I could do something in return for what he's done for me."

"I think he's been a lonely man for most of his life. When you are so brilliant and so insightful about people, you can fast become cynical about the human race's motives. With us, he has a great group of friends, intelligent conversation, and we stretch his mind. We don't have his financial resources, but you can meet him on an intellectual and trustworthy level that makes you invaluable. I've really enjoyed his companionship since we've been dating. What's more is, I think we both enjoy the miles between us as neither of us wants a full-time partner. I've got some coursework papers to grade, so I'm going to take some computer time to get that done," Marie said, settling into the sofa with a mug of coffee.

Jill decided she would sneak back into her bedroom and get dressed without waking Nathan up. She wanted to go outside and explore the property in daylight, and her nightclothes weren't warm enough for that. She was back downstairs with a jacket and ready to go out the front door, when Marie asked, "Should you go out front with a sniper on the loose gunning for you? No pun intended."

Jill stopped for a moment and thought, and then said, "I'm going to have faith in Henrik's team. I bet they've been surveilling the property as we slept. They'll come to fetch me if I'm in danger."

Marie shook her head, thinking she wouldn't use that logic, but she could understand Jill's need for fresh air.

Jill stepped out the front door and looked around for any cars parked on the street with someone in them. The street was empty and then she saw a sign in French that she thought said 'no overnight parking'. Thank you, Montréal, for making it easier for her to spot bad guys. She walked toward the front fence to get a look at the neighborhood and the other beautiful houses. A woman was walking up the street with a large dog that looked like a black wet mop. Jill's curiosity and love of dogs overcame her impulse to worry about her own security. She quickly searched her mind for French greetings. The best she could do was "Bonjour".

The woman answered back with an accent that Jill was unable to detect the origin of. She didn't know how to conduct a conversation in French about a dog, so she just asked in English.

"What a beautiful dog. What kind of breed is that? It's sort of looks like a Giant Schnauzer."

"She's a Black Russian Terrier, well suited for this climate."

"Oh," said Jill backing away when she heard the word, Russian. She turned back and muttered, "Have a nice day," and so missed the gesture of the woman throwing her hand in the air.

Jill went back inside the house, berating herself for her arrogance in approaching the front gate. She felt her phone vibrate and pulled it out to find a message from Henrik.

'Come to the guesthouse, please, and don't say anything.'

She walked through the house and exited into the backyard, taking a look at the concrete walls surrounding the backyard. She didn't see any squirrels playing on them, and thought it was unlikely because they would fall over dead if they touched the electric current,

Henrik and one of his men met her at the door to the guesthouse holding a finger to his lips in a universal gesture of silence. His man held out a scanner and proceeded to scan the backside of Jill. She watched the lights change colors, indicating that he found something. He took out a roll of duct tape and brushed it down the outside of her coat back and sleeves. He ran the scanner again, and it beeped this time at her hair. She hoped he wasn't planning to use the duct tape on her hair as that would be a disaster. Instead, he pulled out a comb and handed it to her. She combed her hair thoroughly and then handed him the comb. He ran the scanner over the comb, and again it lit up, while a scan of her hair was quiet.

Henrik held open what Jill assumed was a lead-lined bag, and his man dropped the duct tape and comb into it. He then scanned it and Jill to make sure that all was good. He nodded.

"We watched you approach the front fence and talk to the woman walking the dog. We listened in to your conversation and saw you flinch when the breed of the dog was revealed. What you missed when you turned your back to return to the house, was a gesture by the woman who threw some of those small listening devices on you. By the time you entered the front door, a car had come by and picked her and the dog up. You're clear now, and better still, we have some insight into the strategy of the Russians. While we're out and about today, we'll do periodic searches in case any additional particles get dropped on us."

"Thanks for watching out for me," Jill said, wondering when she could relax around dogs again. She loved dogs. Her beloved Dalmatian, Trixie, was back home in California with a friend. It was very sneaky of the Russians to lower her defenses by bringing out a dog.

Another one of Henrik's team looked up from a computer he was studying and said, "The woman's name is Natalya Belova, and she is an employee of the Russian Embassy in Ottawa."

"She didn't do anything illegal, so there's nothing to show the police. However, it's interesting and perhaps terrifying that they pulling in Embassy employees to help with this operation. It's not a good sign. Do you know where the Philharmonic conductor is at the moment?" Jill asked.

"No, we're not tracking him. I would think you would have to ask your CIA or the Canadian Special Forces that information as I bet they're tracking him now," Henrik replied.

Jill nodded and said, "I promised Mom that I wasn't going to do any work on the case today. I'm going to enjoy being a tourist. So, who cares where the conductor is," Jill said as she turned to leave the guest house.

As she left, she heard Henrik taking various bets with his staff at how long she would hold out. She just smiled and put the Russians out of her mind. It was time to delve into the history of the region she was in.

They all enjoyed the most peaceful day as tourists they had experienced since the murder at the church. The art museum was magnificent, the park spectacular with the fall colors, and Jill considered the walking tour of Old Montréal educational as she learned much about the history of the city and the province. As an American, she couldn't recall reading that much about Canadian history, and yet the two countries were tied together.

Nathan cooked an Italian dinner paired with great wines while Hope made Jill's favorite dessert – crème brûlée. As they were lounging about the living room, they discussed their plans for the next day in Québec City. They would journey there in Henrik's plane more for its time-saving ability, then the security of the group. They had their tourist attractions lined up for the following day. They would all fly home the following day to the respective states and countries. With their next get-together planned in a few weeks for a Green Bay Packers game.

CHAPTER 22

They left for the Montréal airport the next morning with the plan to arrive for breakfast in a café inside the walled city of Québec City after the short plane ride. What they didn't see was a drone in the middle of the night, dropping the listening devices on the property. While it wasn't much help in hearing their conversations inside the house, there was enough conversation outside that the Russians knew their destination.

As they approached the Québec airport, Jill received a call from Officer Simpson.

"Yes?" What more could she say to a man she didn't want to hear from.

"I understand you're about to land at the Québec City Airport."

"Yes," Jill had an impulse to ask how did he know, but he was the CIA after all.

"Our Russian friends know that too and have followed you there. We need a plan."

"That's for sure. I want you and your counterpart in Canada, and all the police forces between Toronto and here to protect my friends and me. Are we being bugged at the moment? What's your plan?"

Jill wondered how her own CIA knew what the Russians were up to, but she really didn't care. She just wanted a safe environment for her friends. Jill had a slight bump in her seat as the plane touched down.

"Should we stay on the plane?"

"We have a plan, but it's not entirely in place yet. We have a helicopter that will land near your jet to take you on a tour of the city. That will give us time to set up an operation that will sweep all of the Russians up and yet keep you safe."

"I don't like helicopters, so I'll stay aboard the plane with anyone else that doesn't want to go. I'm sure we can make it look like we all boarded the helicopter."

"That will work. The helicopter company is parked in a different area of the airport, and so we have a van coming to fetch you. I think there's a hangar you can wait at nearby. If someone is watching with binoculars, we need you to make it look real."

"Can they blow us out of the sky?"

"No, and they can't get you with a sniper rifle as it's too far away."

"Okay. Keep me informed of what we're doing. We did want to see this city."

Jill ended the call and then looked at her friends aboard the jet as well as Henrik's security detail.

"I don't know how, but the CIA just said the Russians followed us here. He's working with his Canadian counterparts to set up an operation that will keep us safe and collect all the Russians. He needs time to put it in place, and so in the meanwhile for cover, he wants us to take a helicopter tour of Québec City. There's a helicopter awaiting us and a van that will take us there. Personally, I don't like helicopters, so I'm going to stay inside the hangar while you folks enjoy your tour. I just need to enter one side of the copter and get out the other side, so it looks like I'm on board, since it's me that they want to kill the most."

In the end, it was Henrik's security detail that stayed behind with Jill, everyone else was excited for the city tour courtesy of the CIA."

Once the copter lifted off, she called Simpson back.

"Okay, it looks like we're all enjoying an aerial tour of Québec City. My friends were excited to take that tour, so thanks. After this, we were planning breakfast in a French café followed by a walking tour of the walled part of Québec City, along with some historical parks, lunch at the famous riverfront hotel, and a museum visit. What's your plan looking like? Can we still see everything that's on our list?"

"We think so. We want your group to head down a curved and narrow road inside the walled city. Our intent is to have the Russians follow you in the alley, while we pull you in to an interior building and block the exits to the alley. What's the name of the café that you were planning to breakfast at?"

Jill gave him the name and then asked, "Are you sure you'll get them all?"

"No, but at the very least, we'll pick up their sniper."

"You're sure we'll be safe?"

"Very sure, though we may substitute the older woman in your group with someone made up to look like her. We don't want her to get hurt, but we will want your group to walk fast at some point."

"I like that idea. I want her protected. You'll make the substitution?"

"Yes."

"Are you able to keep track of the Russian movements, or only their communications?"

"Just their communications. We did to them what they did to us."

"You dropped some listening devices on their clothing?"

"Yeah."

"Very good," Jill said, clapping her hands in pleasure with this strategy. It felt like the Americans were finally gaining an edge on these Russians. It was about time. "By the way, you met Mr. Klein on the boat. He has a security detail protecting us. They're very good, and should be apprised of your plans as well."

Jill relayed to Henrik's men what the plan was for the day. They nodded and spoke amongst themselves in German. She heard Henrik's name a few times in their discussion, but otherwise, they could've been planning a trip to the moon for all she understood the language.

She settled back and studied the streets of the walled area of Québec City. She could see only one street that might meet their operational needs, and it was in the area of the monastery. Wouldn't that make for a story to tell others – "we were chased through the grounds of a monastery by Russian assassins?" Really, who would believe such a story? She waved over one of Henrik's men and explained her theory, and he agreed with her conclusion.

The helicopter was returning to the hangar, and the rest of her group would be entering the hangar lounge momentarily. She couldn't wait to hear what they thought of the adventure. She heard the rotor blades shut off and then the noise of conversation coming towards her.

"How was the tour?"

"Just thrilling. We saw the nearby snowy mountains, the waterfalls, and we followed the St Lawrence River out to the Atlantic Ocean and saw Newfoundland in the distance. It was fascinating. I'm sure Angela took a ton of pictures for you," Hope said.

"You missed a real treat," Jo said. "It made the shoot-out in the cemetery worth it to get this gift from our government."

"Wow, that's saying a lot. I'm thrilled that the downside of knowing me has brought you this thrilling side trip."

"Why didn't you want to join us?" asked Henrik.

"I was afraid I would toss my cookies."

Henrik looked at her with puzzlement, apparently not having heard that expression before.

She tried again, "I was afraid I would get sick to my stomach and vomit."

"Ah. I had a vision of you trying to hold a tray of cookies as the wind blew in from the helicopter door, and I was going to tell you that the door was closed on the helicopter. You Americans have really interesting expressions."

"Yeah, that's one of my favorites."

"So, where are we going next?" Marie asked. "Hopefully, breakfast is involved."

Jill's cell phone rang then, and she held up her hand. She looked around her, and no one was in the hanger with them other than Henrik's men.

She put her phone on the speaker feature and said, "Yes, Officer Simpson. My friends enjoyed your copter tour, and now we're hoping we're leaving for breakfast. I have you on speaker so we can all hear your plan."

"We've lined up the Sûreté du Québec, which is the Provincial Police Force, Canadian Special Services, and the Québec City Police to run this operation. We are setting up construction signs to block off the street we'll have your group walk down as we don't want civilians in the area that could be taken hostage."

"Is this the area around the monastery?" Jill asked.

"Yes," Simpson said with surprise in his voice.

"We'll keep a watch on the café, it's going to be filled with undercover police officers. We will make the substitution for Mrs. Weber there, and she'll remain behind in the café while the action goes down."

"Why aren't you substituting for all of our team?" Hope asked. "My daughter and her friends should be safe too."

Hope received a silent 'high five' from the group for her question.

"Ma'am, we wouldn't run this operation if we weren't sure that everyone will come out of it alive. We've been after this group of Russians for a long time, and we need to get them in custody, be it in the United States or Canada. Right now, the Canadians have more to arrest them with, than we do. We will be giving the rest of you body armor to wear under your coats as an added precaution. We'll have an officer lead you out of the café, with an upturned umbrella, so she looks like she's a city tour director. Are you ready?"

"And my men?" Henrik asked.

"They should walk with you as your actual protection detail."

"Ah, they have some unusual weapons they could unleash. Should they plan on doing that?"

"Normally, I would say yes, but Canadian laws are different. Let's discuss that in the restaurant. We'll all be there for last-minute questions."

"Okay, then we'll take Henrik's transportation into the city," Jill said, ending the call.

"Sorry Mom, that you won't get to watch the action because there is uneven pavement in the area we're going to, and we wouldn't want you to trip or have to walk very fast at some point."

"I get it, but I don't like it."

"Okay, we'll see you in about twenty minutes at the café," Simpson said.

"Wow, this day has been all about adventure!" Jack said. "I'm coming with you on the next vacation."

Jill relaxed and laugh at his comments, holding her hand up for a group fist bump, she nodded to Marie who said, "All for one," and paused as the group recited back smiling, "One for all."

CHAPTER 23

Twenty minutes later, they were being seated in a restaurant with fabulous breakfast aromas. A waitress, who did not appear to be a cop, took their orders. That was good, as it would mean that they were actually getting some food. It was weird knowing that everyone already seated was there as part of the operation.

A server poured water and said to them, "Each of you needs to get up and head to the bathrooms in the back where we'll outfit you with protective wear," and then looking at Hope said, "Ma'am you'll be here a while, so you'll want to find the bathroom at some point if you drink enough of this wonderful coffee."

Hope laughed at the young man and said, "I'll take my turn last. Marie, you go first."

Fifteen minutes later, they were all sitting at the table looking a little thicker than when they started out that day. Henrik's men were outfitted second, and they had a discussion about the 'weapons' they had with them. Each of them was designed to distract, contain, and identify anyone that assaulted them. They would play a key role in drawing in the Russians into the street, and they had additional armor to account for the added danger.

They finished a wonderful breakfast and got ready to move out. The police had monitors on the surrounding building to watch what the car that tailed them from the airport was up to. A second car arrived with additional men. The Russians saw the Americans, a short time later, one of the Russians strolled past the window to make sure the Americans they sought were dining. They then regrouped about a block away. There were seven of them, six discussing their plan and one stationed around the corner to make sure the Americans didn't leave the restaurant. All of this was relayed inside to the officers planning the next steps.

The monastery was a three-block walk, and if all went as planned, they would be able to resume their vacation unhindered in less than an hour. Better still, they would all be able to head home, and not worry about looking over their shoulders for some very deadly Russians on their tail. The police officer had a wig that roughly imitated Hope's hair, and she borrowed her coat. She made sure to stay inside the pack of friends because anyone that really studied them would realize she was a fake. She hadn't practiced the older woman's gait or other mannerisms. With a final hug between mother and daughter, they were off to meet the police officer outside, holding the umbrella, looking like their tour guide. She pulled out headsets that Jill often saw tourists wearing so they could hear the words of the tour guide without the tour guide shouting. She also showed them a map and showed everyone the layout of the city and took a moment to make sure that while they were looking at the map, they were also doing a sound check on their microphones and speakers.

Okay, Jill thought, this was getting serious. She quickly reviewed in her head as to whether there was anyway around this plan with her and her friends as bait, but she couldn't think of anything. They had planned very well on short notice, though she wasn't sure who all the 'they' were.

They began their walk toward the monastery looking around

them and Henrik's men looking like the protectors they were in real life. They had two blocks to go, and were notified that the Russians were on the move toward them, studying their own maps as they walked. Through the headsets, they heard that the Russians had Makarov semi-automatic pistols that could carry up to twelve bullets each. Some of them had suppressors on them. Simpson explained that it was a gun that was no longer made in Russia, but rather elsewhere in the world. It had popular use in Russia, and its accuracy was fifty-five yards, so they would need to close in. They likely switched from sniper rifles to pistols, as they couldn't conceal the rifles in their clothing like they could with the pistols.

They paused at the bottom on a street that had a slight uphill grade. They would walk up that street and hustle around the corner and through a doorway that was about ten yards in. The door would slam closed, and a lead screen would be rolled across the inside of the front door in case the Russians decided to shoot their way in. Jill saw someone with a road maintenance sign around an underground utility cover. A man seemed to monitor something down below. Jill assumed he was another undercover police officer ready to draw on the Russians. He would have an excellent ability to shoot people in the ankles. She was tempted to look up, on the roofs, but didn't want to give away the plan by looking for law enforcement.

Their leader did a last-minute check. She pointed to the monastery and spoke like she was giving the history of it, instead she was repeating last-minute instructions.

"We'll walk around the corner ahead and on your left just around the corner is a door that will be open, run inside and keep going to the back of the house. Officers inside will handle getting a lead screen in the way. Outside, agents and officers will be arresting a party of seven. We have a Russian interpreter ready to go with a PA to shout instructions. Enter the house at a run and move to the back of it. Do not slow down just because you crossed the threshold, there will be others behind you trying to reach safety. Are we clear?"

The group nodded back to her, and anyone watching them must have thought she was describing a horrible incident that occurred in the monastery based on the expressions on their faces. They began their meandering walk uphill. It was hard to hold down their speed, as they all had the urge to just reach safety. However, a glare from the police officer/tour guide slowed their pace when Marie would have stepped out in front. They received word that the Russians were closing in. They were wearing ballcaps and kerchiefs clearly designed to hide their faces.

They reached the corner and began sprinting for the safety of the door. As they reached the back of the house, they each rushed to count in their heads that everyone was inside. There was a quick moment of relaxation, then they heard glass break in the front and frenzied noise outside. They remained at the back of the house for perhaps twenty minutes while all the activity occurred out on the street. Even though they appeared to be safe, Henrik's men continued to be the barrier between them and the front door. Jill had to admire their dedication to duty.

Twenty minutes after they were hustled into the house, they were free to go. The Russians had been successfully captured. The decoy for Hope returned her coat to Angela, and the Americans headed back to the café. Hope had been informed by a cadet sitting with her, that everyone was safe with not so much as a hair out of place. It was a very anticlimactic end to a busy morning. They resumed their vacation this time with a real guide to this area of Québec City. They all had a secret smile when the guide made to turn up the same street they'd walked an hour ago with the Russians on their heels only to find the street closed and a policeman stationed there. They had quite a crime scene to document and clean up. Someone would be paying for repairs to the building they took cover in as it had to have been damaged by bullets.

With all the worry of the Russians off their shoulders, it was a boisterous group of Germans and Americans enjoying their last day together on their Canadian vacation. They hopped back aboard the plane later that evening to return to Montréal. Officer Simpson scheduled a conference call with Jill late that evening to give her as much a wrap-up as he was allowed to give.

They were gathered on the sofas in the living room with their favorite libations in hand. Henrik's security men had one eye on the outdoor cameras and the other on the group. The danger might be over, but they would escort their boss back home to Germany to make sure he stayed safe. They liked him as a boss and a person.

Jill's phone rang at the appointed time. She was happy to hear that the only injuries were to two Russians who had attempted to escape and had been shot in the lower leg by the policeman hiding in the manhole cover. They recovered enough illegal guns to keep the Russians in jail for that alone for quite some time. Andrei Tamm was confirmed to have the red oil of the cocobolo plant on his hands. In time, he admitted to killing the piano player as life in a Canadian prison couldn't be any worse than being permanently stationed to a Gulag in Siberia. The Symphony Conductor and Mrs. Chernov had joined with Andrei's merry band of Russian thugs to try and take out the Americans. The Toronto Philharmonic had a special performance in Québec City and was now searching for a new conductor. Anna had left the mascara and lipstick behind at the embassy and traveled with the conductor to Québec City, expecting to be needed for the Russian operation. Moscow, which had a habit of triple dealing, never bothered to tell Andrei Tamm until she showed up with the conductor at the airport. The entire group of Russians would spend the next year or so being interviewed by the American and Canadian Global Intelligence sources.

EPILOGUE

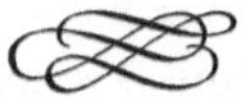

A few weeks later, the tailgate was in place, and Marie left to meet Henrik, where the taxis dropped people off near the stadium. She waited at the curb bundled up in a winter parka. Hat and gloves were green and gold with the name 'Packers' sewn on them. She wore fleece-lined boots over jeans covering her thermal underwear. Still, it was a beautiful day, and she was anxious to be reunited with Henrik, even if it was for a short time. They snatched brief moments of togetherness when their travels permitted, and they were both content with that arrangement.

She saw his hand wave out the window of a taxi in line to drop off its passengers and waved back to him, waiting for the car to approach.

When he exited the taxi carrying a canvas bag, she threw her arms around him for a kiss and then grabbed his hand to lead him to their party.

"I've never seen anything like this," Henrik said as he looked around in wonder at the crowd. Despite the cold temperatures, food was being cooked, people were playing games, and he saw some of the strangest arrays of green and gold clothing in his life.

He pointed to a triangle foam hat that people had on their heads and asked, "What's that?"

"It's a cheesehead. Wisconsin is America's dairyland, and we make a lot of cheese in this state. In the 1980s, the people from the state of Illinois called us the derogatory name 'cheesehead' during a baseball series between our team and theirs. But we didn't consider it derogatory at all and began making cardboard cheese-heads, then it became made out of foam. Then it expanded to cheese-butts and cheese-bras, but it is too cold today to see those items unless some women drink too much and take off their tops, which is possible."

"Really? People have bare skin in this cold?"

"Their blood alcohol levels overcome their common sense. I'm sure you'll see some young men take off their coats and shirts sometime during the game, and it will be caught on camera."

"I shiver just to think about it," Henrik said, stopping to glance at a variety of weird vehicles painted in the theme colors. "I can't think of a sporting event I've ever attended, that looks like this."

They arrived at the tailgate to find their friends with beers in hand, playing a board game of cornhole toss.

After hugs were exchanged, Henrik opened his canvas bag and said, "This is my contribution to the party. It seemed appropriate after our last time together. These are Russian beef Pirozhki, and then he pulled out a small cooler that also contained seven neatly stacked bottles of a Russian beer brand – Stary Melnick."

"So, we get to eat and drink what our Russian enemies sitting in a Canadian jail can no longer have? I love the irony of your selections," Jill said.

"This beer is supposed to taste like your Budweiser. While vodka is more Russian, I knew you would be drinking beer here," Henrik said, passing a bottle to each.

"Cheers! And here's to great friends, good food, and the Green Bay Packers," Angela said, and they all clanked their bottles together.

It was a snow globe game. They sat together about twenty rows up on the fifty-yard line in Lambeau Field. Henrik's kinship deepened with his American friends through the sporting event. He saw their usually logical brains leave their heads as they cheered everything their team did. It was cold, but the fluffy snowflakes were pretty. A player even made a snow angel after he scored. He was trying to think of another sport that held games while it snowed, and he couldn't think of one. It added to the magic of the game and the day.

He noted to himself to make a plan each year to stop by the fabled stadium and catch a game. It was like being at a World Cup final game in which Germany was playing. He couldn't begin to imagine this kind of passion for a team through all kinds of weather in such a small town. Perhaps that was the charm of it all – just everyday people living their lives but united in cheering on the town as represented by its football team. Yes, indeed, this was the life to live.

The End

ABOUT THE AUTHOR

I reside in Northern California with my rescue dog and cat. I love to travel, play sports, read, and drink wine and beer. I enjoy the diversity of the world and I'm always watching people and events for story ideas. All of my stories are generated by my imagination, I don't use AI to write books.

If you would like to sign up for my bi-weekly blog and announcement of new books, please follow this link: https://www.AlecPecheBooks.com

While you're waiting for the next story, if you would be so kind as to leave a review for this book, that would be great. I appreciate all the feedback and support. Reviews buoy my spirits and stoke the fires of creativity.

Readers that sign up for my blog receive a free prequel novelette for the Jill Quint Series.

ALSO BY ALEC PECHE

<u>Jill Quint, MD Forensic Pathologist Series</u>

Time's Up (prequel short story)

Vials

Chocolate Diamonds

A Breck Death

Death On A Green

A Taxing Death

Murder At The Podium

Castle Killing

Crescent City Murder

Sicilian Murder

Opus Murder

Forensic Murder

Return to the Scene of the Crime (short story)

Embers of Murder

Ashes to Murder

Mint Death

<u>Damian Green Series</u>

Red Rock Island

Willow Glen Heist

The Girl From Diana Park

Evergreen Valley Murder

Long Delayed Justice

<u>Michelle Watson Series</u>

Now You Don't See Me

Where Did She Go?

How Did She Get There?

<u>Dog Humor</u>

Eat, Play, Poop: Letters to my parents from camp

<u>New Urban Fantasy Series - Stephanie Jones</u>

The Awakening at Lake Tahoe (short story)

Witch's Medicine (2024)